Thomas Parnell

Poetical Works - Containing Those Published by Mr. Pope

Together with his Whole Posthumous Pieces - Vol. 1

Thomas Parnell

Poetical Works - Containing Those Published by Mr. Pope
Together with his Whole Posthumous Pieces - Vol. 1

ISBN/EAN: 9783337126490

Printed in Europe, USA, Canada, Australia, Japan

Cover: Foto ©Andreas Hilbeck / pixelio.de

More available books at **www.hansebooks.com**

THE
POETICAL WORKS

OF

DR. THO. PARNELL.

Containing thofe

PUBLISHED BY MR. POPE,

Together with his whole

POSTHUMOUS PIECES.

IN TWO VOLUMES.

WITH THE LIFE OF THE AUTHOR.

Dignum laude virum Mufa vetat mori.   HOR.

Such were the notes thy once-lov'd Poet fung,
Till Death untimely ftopp'd his tuneful tongue.
Oh! juft beheld and loft! admir'd and mourn'd!
With fofteft manners, gentleft arts, adorn'd!
Blefs'd in each fcience! blefs'd in ev'ry ftrain!
Dear to the Mufe, to HARLEY dear---in vain!
  For him thou oft haft bid the world attend,
Fond to forget the Statefman in the Friend.----
  Abfent or dead, ftill let a friend be dear,
(A figh the abfent claims, the dead a tear)
Recall thofe nights that clos'd thy toilfome days,
Still hear thy PARNELL in his living lays.----
              POPE TO LORD OXFORD.

VOL. I.

EDINBURG:

AT THE Apollo Prefs, BY THE MARTINS.
Anno 1778.

THE
POETICAL WORKS

OF

DR. THOMAS PARNELL.

VOL. I.

CONTAINING HIS

ANACREONTICS,	HYMNS,
ECLOGUES,	EPISTLES,
SONGS,	MISCELLANIES,

&c. &c. &c.

Charm'd with a zeal the Maker's praise to show,
Bright Gift of Verse descend! and here below
My ravish'd heart with rais'd affection fill,
And warbling o'er the foul incline my will.
Among thy pomp let rich Expression wait,
Let ranging Numbers form thy train complete.----
And when thy feet with gliding beauty tread,
Let Fancy's flow'ry spring erect its head.----
   My call is favour'd, Time, from first to last,
Unwinds his years; the present sees the past:
I view the circles as he turns them o'er,
And fix my footsteps where he went before.
                              GIFT OF POETRY.

EDINBURG:

AT THE Apollo Press, BY THE MARTINS.

Anno 1778.

Dr. THOMAS PARNELL.

Of our exalted Poet, whofe life, though far from being popular, did not altogether pafs in privacy, we
meet with few other accounts than fuch as the life of
every man will afford, *viz.* when he was born, where
he was educated, and where he died; for as the fame
of a fcholar is acquired in folitude, his life feldom
abounds with adventure. But as we are naturally fond
of talking of thofe who have afforded us pleafure,
and as we never receive pleafure without a defire to
be acquainted with the fource from whence it fprings,
it is hoped thefe fimple Memoirs of the man will not
be unacceptable to thofe who admire the poet.

The city of Dublin had the honour of giving birth
to the Author of the following Poems in the 1676,
where Mr. Parnell alfo received the firft rudiments
of his education at the fchool of Dr. Jones. Our
Author was defcended from an ancient family, fettled for fome centuries at Congleton in Chefhire. His
father, who was alfo named Thomas, went over to
Ireland upon the Reftoration, being attached to the
Commonwealth party: in that kingdom he acquired
very confiderable property in lands, which eftates,
as well as thofe he poffeffed in Chefhire, defcended
to our Poet as his eldeft fon.

Our Author was received a member of the College

of Dublin at the age of thirteen, which is much earlier than ufual, as at that univerfity they are ftricter in their examination for admiffion than either at Oxford or Cambridge. His progrefs through the college courfe of ftudy was probably marked with but little fplendour: but it is certain that as a claffical fcholar few could equal him; and this his own compofitions, joined to the deference paid him by the moft eminent men of his time, put beyond a doubt.

In July 1700 he took the degree of Mafter of Arts, and that fame year was ordained a Deacon by William Bifhop of Derry, having obtained a difpenfation from the Primate, as being under twenty-three years of age. About the 1703 or 1704, he was admitted into prieft's orders by William Archbifhop of Dublin; and in February 1705, he was collated by Sir George Afhe, Bifhop of Clogher, to the Archdeaconry of Clogher.

Prior to this date our Author had paid his addreffes to a young lady of great merit and beauty; this lady was Mifs Anne Minchin, whom he married much about this period. He had by her two fons and one daughter. Both the fons died young; but the daughter is ftill alive. His wife died fome time before him, and her death is faid to have made fo great an impreffion on his fpirits, as to be greatly inftrumental in haftening his own. In May 1716 he was prefented by Archbifhop King to the Vicarage of Finglas, a benefice in the Diocefe of Dublin worth about 400 l.

per annum; but he lived not long to enjoy the benefits of this preferment; for in July 1718, when on his way to Ireland, he died at Chester, and was buried in Trinity Church in that city, without any monument to dignify the place of his interment. Having died without male-issue, his estate devolved to his only nephew, Sir John Parnell, Baronet, whose faher was younger brother to the Archdeacon, and one of the Justices of the King's Bench in Ireland.

It frequently happens to men of genius, that no Memoirs can be collected of consequence enough to be recorded by the biographer. A poet, while living, is seldom an object sufficiently great to attract much attention; his real merits are commonly known but to a few, and these are generally sparing of their praises : and when his fame is transmitted to posterity by time, it becomes too late to investigate the transactions of his life, or peculiarities of his disposition.

Dr. Parnell, by what the learned have been able to trace out concerning him, was the most capable man in the world to promote the happiness of those with whom he conversed, but the least qualified to secure his own : his life was wholly spent in agony or rapture; and he was consequently either greatly elated or totally depressed. But the violence of those passions only affected his own quiet, and never interrupted the tranquillity of his connexions and friends; for being extremely sensible of the ridicule of his own

character, he fuccefsfully raifed the mirth of his companions as well at his vexations as at his triumphs.

In his converfation he is faid to have been extremely
engaging, though in what its chiefeft excellence con-
fifted is at prefent unknown. Even before he difco-
vered any genius in literary purfuits, his friendfhip
was courted by perfons of all ranks and parties. The
letters which were addreffed to him by his friends and
correfpondents are full of compliments upon his talents as a companion, and his good nature as a man.
Pope ftands foremoft in the lift of thofe who bear this
teftimony to the focial qualities of Parnell, and feems
to regret his abfence more than any of the reft. One
of his letters is in the following words :

Dear Sir,   *London, July* 29.

" I wish it were not as ungenerous as vain to com-
" plain too much of a man that forgets me, but I could
" expoftulate with you a whole day upon your inhu-
" man filence; I call it inhuman, nor would you think
" it lefs, if you were truly fenfible of the uneafinefs it
" gives me. Did I know you fo ill as to think you
" proud, I would be much lefs concerned than I am
" able to be, when I know one of the beft-natured
" men alive neglects me; and if you know me fo ill
" as to think amifs of me, with regard to my friend-
" fhip for you, you really do not deferve half the
" trouble you occafion me. I need not tell you that

" both Mr. Gay and myself have written several let-
" ters in vain; that we are constantly inquiring of
" all who have seen Ireland if they saw you, and that
" (forgotten as we are) we are every day remembering
" you in our most agreeable hours. All this is true,
" as that we are sincerely lovers of you, and deplo-
" rers of your absence, and that we form no wish more
" ardently than that which brings you over to us,
" and places you in your old seat between us. We
" have lately had some distant hopes of the Dean's
" design to revisit England; will not you accompany
" him? or is England to lose every thing that has
" any charms for us? and must we pray for banish-
" ment as a benediction?——I have once been witness
" of some, I hope all, of your splenetic hours; come
" and be a comforter in your turn to me in mine. I
" am in such an unsettled state, that I can't tell if I
" shall ever see you, unless it be this year; whether
" I do or not, be ever assured you have as large a
" share of my thoughts and good wishes as any man,
" and as great a portion of gratitude in my heart as
" would enrich a monarch, could he know where to
" find it. I shall not die without testifying something
" of this nature; and leaving to the world a memo-
" rial of the friendship that has been so great a plea-
" sure and a pride to me. It would be like writing
" my own epitaph, to acquaint you what I have lost
" since I saw you, what I have done, what I have

" thought, where I have lived, and where I now re-
" pofe in obfcurity. My friend Jervas, the bearer of
" this, will inform you of all particulars concerning
" me, and Mr. Ford is charged with a thoufand loves,
" and a thoufand complaints, and a thoufand com-
" miffions, to you on my part: they will both tax you
" with the negleȼt of fome promifes which were too
" agreeable to us all to be forgot : if you care for any
" of us, tell them fo, and write fo to me. I can fay
" no more, but that I love you, and am, in fpite of
" the longeft negleȼt or abfence, Dear Sir,

   " Your moft faithful affeȼtionate friend and fervant,

      " A. POPE.

   " Gay is in Devonfhire, and from thence goes to
" Bath. My father and mother never fail to com-
" memorate you."

To this fondnefs which Pope fhowed for the company and correfpondence of Parnell, he alfo owed
him feveral literary obligations for the affiftance given
him in his tranflation of Homer. But Gay was obli-
gated to our Author upon a different fcore; for his
finances being generally low, he was not above re-
ceiving at Parnell's hands (whom want did not com-
pel into the fervice of the Mufes, but who appeared
in their train from genius and inclination) the copy-
money which the latter got for his writings. The
reader will not be difpleafed to fee fome letters under

the hands of Pope and Gay in proof of what is here
advanced.

Dear Sir,   *Binfield, near Oakingham, Tuef.*
" I believe the hurry you were in hindered your
" giving me a word by the laſt poſt, ſo that I am
" yet to learn whether you got well to Town, or con-
" tinue ſo there. I very much fear both for your
" health and your quiet, and no man living can be
" more truly concerned in any thing that touches
" either than myſelf. I would comfort myſelf, how-
" ever, with hoping that your buſineſs may not be
" unſuccefsful for your ſake, and that, at leaſt, it
" may ſoon be put into other proper hands. For my
" own, I beg earneſtly of you to return to us as ſoon
" as poſſible. You know how very much I want you,
" and that however your buſineſs may depend upon
" any other, my buſineſs depends entirely upon you;
" and yet ſtill I hope you will find your man, even
" though I loſe you the mean while. At this time,
" the more I love you the more I can ſpare you,
" which alone will, I dare ſay, be a reaſon to you to
" let me have you back the ſooner. The minute I loſt
" you, Euſtathins with nine hundred pages, and nine
" thouſand contractions of the Greek character, aroſe
" to my view! Spendanus, with all his auxiliaries, in
" number a thouſand pages, (value three ſhillings)
" and Dacier's three volumes, Barne's two, Valterie's

" three, Cuperus, half in Greek, Leo Allatius, three
" parts in Greek, Scaliger, Macrobius, and (worfe
" than them all) Aulus Gellius! All thefe rufhed upon
" my foul at once, and whelmed me under a fit of the
" headach. I curfed them all religioufly; damned
" my beft friends among the reft, and even blaf-
" phemed Homer himfelf. Dear Sir, not only as you
" are a friend, and a good-natured man, but as you
" are a Chriftian and a divine, come back fpeedily,
" and prevent the increafe of my fins; for at the rate
" I have begun to rave, I fhall not only damn all the
" poets and commentators who have gone before
" me, but be damned myfelf by all who come after
" me. To be ferious, you have not only left me to
" the laft degree impatient for your return, who at
" all times fhould have been fo, (though never fo
" much as fince I knew you in beft health here) but
" you have wrought feveral miracles upon our fami-
" ly: you have made old people fond of a young and
" gay perfon, and inveterate Papifts of a clergyman-
" of the Church of England : even nurfe herfelf is in
" danger of being in love in her old age, and (for all-
" I know) would even marry Dennis for your fake,
" becaufe he is your man, and loves his mafter. In
" fhort, come down forthwith, or give me good rea-
" fons for delaying, though but for a day or two, by
" the next poft. If I find them juft I will come up-
" to you, though you know how precious my time is

" at prefent. My hours were never worth fo much
" money before; but perhaps you are not fenfible of
" this, who give away your own works. You are a
" generous author; I a hackney fcribbler: you are a
" Grecian, and bred at an univerfity; I a poor Eng-
" lifhman, of my own educating: you are a reverend
" perfon; I a wag: in fhort, you are Dr. Parnelle, (with
" an e at the end of your name) and I

" Your moft obliged

" and affectionate friend,

" and faithful fervant,

" A. POPE."

" My hearty fervice to the Dean, Dr Arbuthnot,
" Mr Ford, and the true genuine fhepherd, J. Gay
" of Devon. I expect him down with you."

It appears pretty clear from the above that Parnell fhared with Pope in the labours of his tranflations, although the epiftle is fo ambiguoufly worded
as to render a direct charge of this in fome meafure
impoffible. He is, however, more explicit in regard
to his friend Gay's obligations to our Author. His
words, in a letter without date, are to the following
purpofe:

Dear Sir,
" I WRITE to you with the fame warmth, the fame
" zeal of good-will and friendfhip, with which I ufed

" to converse with you two years ago, and can't
" think myself absent when I feel you so much at
" my heart. The picture of you which Jervas brought
" me over is infinitely less lively a representation
" than that I carry about with me, and which rises
" to my mind whenever I think of you. I have many
" an agreeable reverie through those woods and downs
" where we once rambled together: my head is some-
" times at the Bath, and sometimes at Letcomb,
" where the Dean makes a great part of my imagi-
" nary entertainment; this being the cheapest way
" of treating me, I hope he will not be displeased at
" this manner of paying my respects to him, instead
" of following my friend Jervas' example, which, to
" say the truth, I have as much inclination to do as
" I want ability. I have been ever since December
" last in greater variety of business than any such
" man as you (that is, divines and philosophers) can
" possibly imagine a reasonable creature capable of.
" Gay's play, among the rest, has cost much time
" and long-suffering, to stem a tide of malice and
" party that certain authors have raised against it.
" The best revenge upon such fellows is now in my
" hands; I mean your Zoilus, which really transcends
" the expectation I had conceived of it. I have put
" it into the press, beginning with the poem Batra-
" chom; for you seem, by the first paragraph of the
" Dedication to it, to design to prefix the name of

" fome particular perfon. I beg, therefore, to know
" for whom you intend it, that the publication may
" not be delayed on this account; and this as foon
" as is poffible. Inform me, alfo, upon what terms I
" am to deal with the bookfeller, and whether you
" defign the *copy-money for Gay*, as you formerly
" talked; what number of books you would have
" yourfelf, *&c.* I fcarce fee any thing to be altered
" in this whole piece. In the Poems you fent I will
" take the liberty you allow me. The ftory of Pan-
" dora, and the Eclogue upon Health, are two of the
" moft beautiful things I ever read. I don't fay this
" to the prejudice of the reft, but as I have read thefe
" oftener. Let me know how far my commiffion is to
" extend, and be confident of my punctual perfor-
" mance of whatever you enjoin. I muft add a pa-
" ragraph on this occafion in regard to Mr Ward,
" whofe verfes have been a great pleafure to me: I
" will contrive they fhall be fo to the world, when-
" ever I can find a proper opportunity of publifh-
" ing them.

" I fhall very foon print an entire collection of my
" own Madrigals, which I look upon as making my
" laft will and teftament, fince in it I fhall give all I
" ever intend to give, (which I'll beg your's and the
" Dean's acceptance of) you muft look on me no more
" a poet, but a plain commoner, who lives upon his
" own, and fears and flatters no man. I hope, before

" I die, to difcharge the debt I owe to Homer, and
" get upon the whole juft fame enough to ferve for
" an annuity for my own time, though I leave no-
" thing to pofterity.

" I beg our correfpondence may be more frequent
" than it has been of late. I am fure my efteem and
" love for you never more deferved it from you, or
" more prompted it from you. I defired our friend
" Jervas (in the greateft hurry of my bufinefs) to fay
" a great deal in my name, both to yourfelf and the
" Dean, and muft once more repeat the affurances to
" you both of an unchanging friendfhip and unalter-
" able efteem. I am, Dear Sir, moft entirely

" Your affectionate,

" faithful, obliged friend and fervant,

" A. POPE."

It is apparent from thefe letters of Pope to Parnell,
that our Author was a benevolent and fincere man.
He was ftudious that his friends fhould always fee
him to the beft advantage; for when he felt the ap-
proaches of fpleen and uneafinefs, to which he was
liable, and which fometimes perfecuted him for weeks
together, he returned with expedition to the remoter
parts of Ireland, and there indulged in the gloomy
fatisfaction of exhibiting hideous paintings of the folitude to which he had retired. Scarce a bog in his

neighbourhood was left without reproach, *and scarce a mountain rear'd its head unsung.* And hence, replies Pope, in answer to one of these dreary descriptions from Parnell, " We are both miserably enough situ-
" ated, God knows; but of the two evils I think the
" solitudes of the south are to be preferred to the
" deserts of the west."

What Parnell permitted the world to see of his life was splendid, his fortune being very considerable; the fact, however, is, that he lived to the extent of it, and his expenses exceeding his annual income, his succes-
for found the estate somewhat impaired at his decease. It was the practice of our Author, on collecting his yearly revenues, to set out for England, there to en-
joy the company of his friends, and laugh at the more prudent part of the world employed in pursuits after wealth. Those select friends were Swift, Pope, Arbuthnot, Gay, and Jervas. Lord Oxford was also a-
mong the number of Parnell's intimate friends, whom Pope has complimented on the delicacy of his choice in the following elegant lines :

> For him thou oft haft bid the world attend,
> Fond to forget the Statesman in the Friend ;
> For Swift and him despis'd the farce of state,
> The sober follies of the wife and great ;
> Dext'rous the craving fawning crowd to quit,
> And pleas'd to 'scape from Flattery to Wit.

The Scriblerus Club, of which Swift, Pope, Gay, Arbuthnot, and Jervas, together with our Author,

were the principal members, wrote many things in
conjunction, and Gay ufually held the pen : but there
is fomething feeble and quaint in all their attempts,
as if company repreffed thought, and genius wanted
folitude for its boldeft and happieft exertions. Of
thofe performances in which Parnell had the principal fhare, that of the Origin of the Sciences from the
monkies in Ethiopia is particularly mentioned by
Pope himfelf in fome manufcript anecdotes which he
left behind him. The life of Homer, as prefixed to
Pope's tranflation of the Iliad, is the work of Parnell, but corrected by the tranflator, who affures the
world the corrections were not effected without great
labour. Parnell's profe writings teem with imagina-
tion, and fhew great learning, but they want that
fweetnefs and eafe for which his poetry is fo much
diftinguifhed.

There have been few poetical focieties more talked
of, or that have produced a greater variety of whim-
fical conceits, than this of the Scriblerus Club, the
members of which, when in Town, were feldom afun-
der. Swift was ufually the butt of the company, and
if a trick was intended, it was generally at the expenfe of the Dean of St. Patrick's. The whole party
once agreed to walk to the houfe of Lord B———,
whofe feat is about a dozen miles from Town; and as
it was agreed by all that each fhould make the beft
of his way, Swift, who was a remarkable walker, foon

left his friends behind him, fully refolved, upon his arrival, as was his cuftom, to make choice of the very beft bed for himfelf. Parnell, determined to fruftrate his intended fcheme, mounting on horfeback, arrived at Lord B———'s by another road, long before Swift. Having apprifed his Lordfhip of the Dean's defign, it was refolved at all events to keep him out of the houfe, but how to effeƈt this was the queftion. Swift, who never had the fmall-pox, dreaded catching that diforder; as foon, therefore, as he appeared ftriding along at fome diftance from the houfe, a meffenger was difpatched to inform him that the fmall-pox raged with great violence in the family, but that there was a fummer-houfe, with a field-bed in it, at his ferrice, at the end of the garden. There the difappointed Dean retired, and fupped on a cold collation fent him from the houfe, while the reft were feafting within. At laft, compaffionating his fituation, he was permitted to join the company, on promife never to chufe the beft bed in future.

How long the Scriblerus Club continued is not eafy to determine; but as the whole of Parnell's poetical exiftence was not of more than eight or ten years' duration, his firft excurfion to England being about the 1706, and he dying in the 1718, it is probable the Club began with him, and that his death put a period to its exiftence: for fuch was the feftivity of his converfation, the benevolence of his heart, and the generofity of his temper, qualities that tend to cement any fociety, that his lofs could hardly be replaced. Thus, in the fpace of a very few years, Parnell attained a fhare of fame equal to what moft of his cotemporaries acquired in a long life.

The death of his wife, it is faid, was a ftroke upon our Author which he was unable to fupport; from which period he could never venture to court the Mufe in folitude, where he was fure to find the image of her who firft infpired his attempts. During his laft years he therefore became more and more folicitous of company, and could fcarcely fupport the thoughts of being alone. He began to throw himfelf into every company, and to feek from wine if not relief, at leaft infenfibility. Thofe helps that forrow firft called in for affiftance habit foon rendered neceffary; and he fell in fome meafure a martyr to conjugal fidelity before the fortieth year of his age.

Parnell is only to be confidered as a Poet, and the univerfal efteem in which his Poems are held, and the reiterated pleafure they give in the perufal, are fufficient evidences of their merit. His poetical language is not lefs correct than his fubjects are pleafing. He is ever happy in the felection of his images, and fcrupuloufly careful in the choice of his fubjects. His writings bear no refemblance to thofe tawdry things which it has for fome time been the fafhion to admire, in writing which the poet fits down without any

plan, and heaps up splendid images without any se-
lection. Our Poet gives out his beauties with a sparing hand; he is still carrying his reader forward, and
just gives him refreshment sufficient to support him to
his journey's end. At the end of his course the reader regrets that his way has been so short; he wonders that it gave him so little trouble, and so resolves
to go the journey over again: for, to use the words of
the celebrated Mr. Hume—Parnell, after the fiftieth
reading, is as fresh as at the first.

Parnell appears to be the last of that great school
that had modelled itself upon the Ancients, and taught
English poetry to resemble what the generality of mankind have allowed to excel. A studious and correct
observer of Antiquity, he set himself to consider Nature
with the lights it lent him, and he found that the
more aid he borrowed from the one, the more de-
lightfully he resembled the other. To copy Nature is
a task the most bungling workman is able to execute;
to select such parts as contribute to delight is reser-
ved only for those whom accident has blessed with
uncommon talents, or such as have read the Ancients with indefatigable industry.

The Poems published in the different Miscellanies
by Parnell, during his life, were after his death collected into one volume, and published by Pope, to
which he prefixed an elegant copy of verses to Lord
Oxford, already mentioned. Besides these Parnell

had written a number of other Poems, moftly on fubjects moral and divine, which were afterwards publifhed under the title of *Pofthumous Works*, having
an advertifement prefixed, which includes an attefta-
tion by the late Dean Swift as to the authenticity of
the Poems. The whole Poems of Parnell, therefore, as
well thofe publifhed by Pope, as thofe comprehended
under the title of his Pofthumous Works, are in-
cluded in the prefent edition. As his Pieces are nu-
merous, and on different fubjects, it would fwell this
Narrative beyond the prefcribed limits to give ftric-
tures on their refpective merits; but the whole have
ever been allowed to be good, and the greater part
of that whole excellent.

ROBERT,

EARL OF OXFORD AND EARL MORTIMER.

Such were the notes thy once-lov'd Poet fung,
Till Death untimely ftopp'd his tuneful tongue.
Oh! juft beheld and loft! admir'd and mourn'd!
With fofteft manners, gentleft arts, adorn'd!
Blefs'd in each fcience! blefs'd in ev'ry ftrain!   5
Dear to the Mufe, to Harley dear——in vain!

  For him thou oft haft bid the world attend,
Fond to forget the Statefman in the Friend;
For Swift and him defpis'd the farce of ftate,
The fober follies of the wife and great;   10
Dextrous the craving fawning crowd to quit,
And pleas'd to 'fcape from Flattery to Wit.

  Abfent or dead, ftill let a friend be dear,
(A figh the abfent claims, the dead a tear)
Recall thofe nights that clos'd thy toilfome days, 15
Still hear thy Parnell in his living lays;
Who carelefs now of int'reft, fame, or fate,
Perhaps forgets that Oxford e'er was great;
Or deeming meaneft what we greateft call,
Beholds thee glorious only in thy fall.   20

  And fure if aught below the feats divine
Can touch immortals, 'tis a foul like thine;

A foul fupreme, in each hard inftance try'd,
Above all pain, all paffion, and all pride,
The rage of pow'r, the blaft of public breath,   25
The luft of lucre, and the dread of death.
   In vain to deferts thy retreat is made,
The Mufe attends thee to thy filent fhade:
'Tis her's the brave man's lateft fteps to trace,
Rejudge his acts, and dignify difgrace.   30
When Int'reft calls off all her fneaking train,
And all the oblig'd defert, and all the vain,
She waits or to the fcaffold or the cell,
When the laft ling'ring friend has bid farewell:
Ev'n now fhe fhades thy ev'ning walk with bays, 35
(No hireling fhe, no proftitute to praife)
Ev'n now, obfervant of the parting ray,
Eyes the calm fun-fet of thy various day,
Through Fortune's cloud one truly great can fee,
Nor fears to tell that Mortimer is he.   40

Sept. 25. 1721.   A. POPE.

ANACREONTIC I.

Wʜᴇɴ spring came on with fresh delight,
To cheer the soul and charm the sight,
While easy breezes, softer rain,
And warmer suns, salute the plain,
'Twas then, in yonder piny grove,   5
That Nature went to meet with Love.

    Green was her robe, and green her wreath,
Where'er she trod 'twas green beneath;
Where'er she turn'd the pulses beat
With new recruits of genial heat;   10
And in her train the birds appear,
To match for all the coming year.

    Rais'd on a bank, where daisies grew,
And vi'lets intermix'd a blue,
She finds the boy she went to find;   15
A thousand Pleasures wait behind ;
Aside a thousand arrows lie,
But all unfeather'd wait to fly.

    When they met, the dame and boy,
Dancing Graces, idle Joy,   20
Wanton Smiles, and airy Play,
Conspir'd to make the scene be gay;

Love pair'd the birds through all the grove,
And Nature bid them sing to Love;
Sitting, hopping, flutt'ring, sing,   25
And pay their tribute from the wing,
To fledge the shafts that idly lie,
And yet unfeather'd wait to fly.

   'Tis thus, when spring renews the blood,
They meet in ev'ry trembling wood,   30
And thrice they make the plumes agree,
And every dart they mount with three,
And ev'ry dart can boast a kind,
Which suits each proper turn of mind.

   From the tow'ring eagle's plume   35
The gen'rous hearts accept their doom;
Shot by the peacock's painted eye
The vain and airy lovers die:
For careful dames and frugal men
The shafts are speckled by the hen.   40
The pyes and parrots deck the darts,
When prattling wins the panting hearts;
When from the voice the passions spring,
The warbling finch affords a wing:
Together by the sparrow stung,   45
Down fall the wanton and the young;
And fledg'd by geese the weapons fly,
When others love they know not why.

   All this (as late I chanc'd to rove)
I learn'd in yonder waving grove.   50

" And fee," fays Love, (who call'd me near)
" How much I deal with Nature here,
" How both fupport a proper part,
" She gives the feather, I the dart:
" Then ceafe for fouls averfe to figh, 55
" If Nature crofs ye, fo do I;
" My weapon there unfeather'd flies,
" And fhakes and fhuffles through the fkies:
" But if the mutual charms I find
" By which fhe links you mind to mind, 60
" They wing my fhafts, I poize the darts,
" And ftrike from both through both your hearts." 62

ANACREONTIC II.

Gay Bacchus, liking Eftcourt's wine,
A noble meal befpoke us,
And for the guefts that were to dine
Brought Comus, Love, and Jocus.

The god near Cupid drew his chair, 5
Near Comus Jocus plac'd,
For wine makes love forget its care,
And mirth exalts a feaft.

The more to pleafe the fprightly god,
Each fweet engaging Grace 10

Put on fome clothes to come abroad,
And took a waiter's place.

Then Cupid nam'd at every glafs
A lady of the fky,
While Bacchus fwore he'd drink the lafs,   15
And had it bumper-high.

Fat Comus tofs'd his brimmers o'er,
And always got the moft;
Jocus took care to fill him more,
Whene'er he mifs'd the toaft.   20

They call'd and drank at every touch;
He fill'd and drank again;
And if the gods can take too much,
'Tis faid they did fo then.

Gay Bacchus little Cupid ftung,   25
By reck'ning his deceits,
And Cupid mock'd his ftamm'ring tongue,
With all his ftagg'ring gaits:

And Jocus droll'd on Comus' ways,
And tales without a jeft,   30
While Comus call'd his witty plays
But waggeries at beft.

Such talk soon set 'em all at odds;
And, had I Homer's pen,
I'd sing ye how they drunk like gods,   35
And how they fought like men.

To part the fray the Graces fly,
Who make 'em soon agree ;
Nay, had the Furies' selves been nigh,
They still were three to three.   40

Bacchus appeas'd, rais'd Cupid up,
And gave him back his bow,
But kept some darts to stir the cup
Where sack and sugar flow.

Jocus took Comus' rosy crown,   45
And gaily wore the prize,
And thrice in mirth he push'd him down,
As thrice he strove to rise.

Then Cupid sought the myrtle grove
Where Venus did recline,   50
And Venus close embracing Love,
They join'd to rail at wine.

And Comus, loudly cursing wit,
Roll'd off to some retreat,

                    C iij

Where boon companions gravely fit
In fat unwieldy ſtate.

Bacchus and Jocus, ſtill behind,
For one freſh glaſs prepare:
They kiſs, and are exceeding kind,
And vow to be ſincere.

But part in time whoever hear
This our inſtructive ſong;
For tho' ſuch friendſhips may be dear,
They can't continue long.

ECLOGUES.

HEALTH.

AN ECLOGUE.

Now early shepherds o'er the meadow pass,
And print long footsteps in the glitt'ring grass;
The cows neglectful of their pasture stand,
By turns obsequious to the milker's hand.
　　When Damon softly trod the shaven lawn,   5
Damon, a youth from city cares withdrawn;
Long was the pleasing walk he wander'd through,
A cover'd arbour clos'd the distant view;
There rests the youth, and while the feather'd throng
Raise their wild music, thus contrives a song.   10
　　Here wafted o'er by mild Etesian air,
Thou country goddess, beauteous Health! repair;
Here let my breast thro' quiv'ring trees inhale
Thy rosy blessings with the morning gale.
What are the fields, or flow'rs, or all I see?   15
Ah! tasteless all, if not enjoy'd with thee.
　　Joy to my Soul! I feel the goddess nigh,
The face of Nature cheers as well as I;
O'er the flat green refreshing breezes run,
The smiling daisies blow beneath the sun,   20
The brooks run purling down with silver waves,
The planted lanes rejoice with dancing leaves,

The chirping birds from all the compafs rove,
To tempt the tuneful echoes of the grove;
High funny fummits, deeply fhaded dales,   25
Thick moffy banks, and flow'ry winding vales,
With various profpect gratify the fight,
And fcatter fix'd attention in delight.

Come, country Goddefs! come; nor thou fuffice,
But bring thy mountain-fifter Exercife.   30
Call'd by thy lively voice fhe turns her pace,
Her winding horn proclaims the finifh'd chace;
She mounts the rocks, fhe fkims the level plain,
Dogs, hawks, and horfes, crowd her early train;
Her hardy face repels the tanning wind,   35
And lines and mefhes loofely flote behind:
All thefe as means of toil the feeble fee,
But thefe are helps to pleafure join'd with thee.

Let Sloth lie foft'ning till high noon in down,
Or lolling fan her in the fult'ry town,   40
Unnerv'd with reft, and turn her own difeafe,
Or fofter others in luxurious eafe:
I mount the courfer, call the deep-mouth'd hounds,
The fox unkennell'd flies to covert grounds;
I lead where ftags thro' tangled thickets tread, 45
And fhake the faplings with their branching head;
I make the falcons wing their airy way,
And foar to feize, or ftooping ftrike, their prey;
To fnare the fifh I fix the luring bait;
To wound the fowl I lead the gun with fate.   50

'Tis thus thro' change of exercife I range,
And ftrength and pleafure rife from ev'ry change.
Here, beauteous Health ! for all the year remain,
When the next comes, I'll charm thee thus again.

   Oh come, thou Goddefs of my rural fong !   55
And bring thy daughter, calm Content, along,
Dame of the ruddy cheek and laughing eye,
From whofe bright prefence clouds of forrow fly :
For her I mow my walks, I plat my bow'rs,
Clip low my hedges, and fupport my flow'rs ;   60
To welcome her this fummer-feat I dreft,
And here I court her when fhe comes to reft ;
When fhe from exercife to learned eafe
Shall change again, and teach the change to pleafe.

   Now friends converfing my foft hours refine,   65
And Tully's Tufculum revives in mine :
Now to grave books I bid the mind retreat,
And fuch as make me rather good than great ;
Or o'er the works of eafy Fancy rove,
Where flutes and innocence amufe the grove :   70
The native bard that on Sicilian plains
Firft fung the lowly manners of the fwains,
Or Maro's Mufe, that in the faireft light
Paints rural profpects and the charms of fight ;
Thefe foft amufements bring content along,   75
And fancy, void of forrow, turns to fong.
Here, beauteous Health ! for all the year remain,
When the next comes, I'll charm thee thus again. 78

THE FLIES.

AN ECLOGUE.

When in the river cows for coolnefs ftand,
And fheep for breezes feek the lofty land,
A youth (whom Æfop taught that ev'ry tree,
Each bird and infeƈt, fpoke as well as he)
Walk'd calmly mufing in a fhaded way,   5
Where flow'ring hawthorn broke the funny ray,
And thus inftruƈts his moral pen to draw
A fcene that obvious in the field he faw.

    Near a low ditch, where fhallow waters meet,
Which never learn'd to glide with liquid feet,   10
Whofe Naïads never prattle as they play,
But, fcreen'd with hedges, flumber out the day,
There ftands a flender fern's afpiring fhade,
Whofe anfw'ring branches regularly laid:
Put forth their anfw'ring boughs, and proudly rife
Three ftories upward in the nether fkies.   16

    For fhelter here, to fhun the noon-day heat,
An airy nation of the Flies retreat;
Some in foft air their filken pinions ply,
And fome from bough to bough delighted fly;   20
Some rife, and circling light to perch again,
A pleafing murmur hums along the plain.
So when a ftage invites to pageant fhows,
(If great and fmall are like) appear the beaux;

In boxes fome with fpruce pretention fit, 25
Some change from feat to feat within the pit,
Some roam the fcenes, or, turning, ceafe to roam;
Preluding mufic fills the lofty dome.
  When thus a Fly (if what a Fly can fay
Deferves attention) rais'd the rural lay: 30
 " Where late Amintor made a nymph a bride,
" Joyful I flew by young Favonia's fide,
" Who, mindlefs of the feafting, went to fip
" The balmy pleafure of the fhepherd's lip:
" I faw the wanton, where I ftoop'd to fup, 35
" And half refolv'd to drown me in the cup,
" Till, brufh'd by carelefs hands, fhe foar'd above:
" Ceafe, Beauty! ceafe to vex a tender love."
  Thus ends the youth, the buzzing meadow rung,
And thus the rival of his mufic fung: 40
 " When funs by thoufands fhone in orbs of dew,
" I, wafted foft, with Zepbyretta flew,
" Saw the clean pail, and fought the milky cheer,
" While little Daphne feiz'd my roving dear.
" Wretch that I was! I might have warn'd the dame,
" Yet fat indulging as the danger came; 46
" But the kind huntrefs left her free to foar:
" Ah! guard, ye Lovers! guard a miftrefs more."
  Thus from the fern, whofe high-projecting arms
The fleeting nation bent with dufky fwarms, 50
The fwains their love in eafy mufic breathe,
When tongues and tumult ftun the field beneath:

Black ants in teams come dark'ning all the road,
Some call to march, and fome to lift the load;
They ftrain, they labour with inceffant pains,   55
Prefs'd by the cumbrous weight of fingle grains.
The Flies, ftruck filent, gaze with wonder down;
The bufy burghers reach their earthy town,
Where lay the burthens of a wint'ry ftore,
And thence unwearied part in fearch of more: · 60
Yet one grave fage a moment's fpace attends,
And the fmall city's loftieft point afcends,
Wipes the falt dew that trickles down his face,
And thus harangues them with the graveft grace:
  " Ye foolifh Nurflings of the fummer air !   65
" Thefe gentle tunes and whining fongs forbear;
" Your trees and whifp'ring breeze, your grove and
" Your Cupid's quiver, and his mother's dove : [love,
" Let bards to bufinefs bend their vig'rous wing,
" And fing but feldom, if they love to fing;   70
" Elfe when the flourets of the feafon fail,
" And this your ferny fhade forfakes the vale,
" Tho' one would fave ye, not one grain of wheat
" Should pay fuch fongfters idling at my gate."
  He ceas'd: the Flies, incorrigibly vain,
Heard the May'r's fpeech, and fell to fing again. 76

SONGS.

SONG I.

Wʜᴇɴ thy beauty appears
In its graces and airs,
All bright as an angel new dropt from the ſky,
At diſtance I gaze, and am aw'd by my fears,
So ſtrangely you dazzle my eye!   5

But when without art
Your kind thoughts you impart,
When your love runs in bluſhes thro' every vein;
When it darts from your eyes, when it pants in your
Then I know you're a woman again.   [heart,

" There's a paſſion and pride   11
" In our ſex (ſhe reply'd)
" And thus (might I gratify both) I would do :
" Still an angel appear to each lover beſide,
" But ſtill be a woman to you."   15

SONG II.

Tʜʏʀsɪs, a young and am'rous ſwain,
Saw two, the beauties of the plain,

Who both his heart fubdue;
Gay Cælia's eyes were dazzling fair,
Sabina's eafy fhape and air   5
With fofter magic drew.

He haunts the ftream, he haunts the grove,
Lives in a fond romance of love,
And feems for each to die,
Till each a little fpiteful grown,   10
Sabina Cælia's fhape ran down,
And fhe Sabina's eye.

Their envy made the fhepherd find
Thofe eyes which Love could only blind,
So fet the lover free :   15
No more he haunts the grove or ftream,
Or with a true-love knot and name
Engraves a wounded tree.

" Ah, Cælia! (fly Sabina cry'd)
" Tho' neither love, we're both deny'd;   20
" Now to fupport the fex's pride,
" Let either fix the dart."
" Poor Girl! (fays Cælia) fay no more;
" For fhould the fwain but one adore,
" That fpite which broke his chains before
" Would break the other's heart."   26

SONG III.

My days have been so wondrous free,
The little birds that fly
With careless ease from tree to tree
Were but as bless'd as I.

Ask gliding waters if a tear   5
Of mine increas'd their stream?
Or ask the flying gales if e'er
I lent one sigh to them?

But now my former days retire,
And I'm by beauty caught;   10
The tender chains of sweet desire
Are fix'd upon my thought.

Ye Nightingales! ye twisting Pines!
Ye Swains that haunt the grove!
Ye gentle Echoes! breezy Winds!   15
Ye close Retreats of Love!

With all of nature, all of art,
Assist the dear design;
O teach a young unpractis'd heart
To make my Nancy mine.   20

The very thought of change I hate
As much as of defpair,
Nor ever covet to be great,
Unlefs it be for her.

'Tis true the paffion in my mind
Is mix'd with foft diftrefs,
Yet while the fair I love is kind,
I cannot wifh it lefs.

HYMNS.

A HYMN TO CONTENTMENT.

Lovely, lasting peace of mind !
Sweet delight of human kind !
Heav'nly born, and bred on high,
To crown the fav'rites of the sky
With more of happiness below   5
Than victors in a triumph know !
Whither, O whither art thou fled,
To lay thy meek contented head !
What happy region dost thou please
To make the seat of calms and ease ?   10
    Ambition searches all its sphere
Of pomp and state to meet thee there.
Increasing Avarice would find
Thy presence in its gold enshrin'd.
The bold advent'rer ploughs his way   15
Thro' rocks, amidst the foaming sea,
To gain thy love, and then perceives
Thou wert not in the rocks and waves.
The silent heart, which grief assails,
Treads soft and lonesome o'er the vales,   20
Sees daisies open, rivers run,
And seeks (as I have vainly done)

Amusing thought, but learns to know
That solitude's the nurse of woe.
No real happiness is found   25
In trailing purple o'er the ground;
Or in a soul exalted high,
To range the circuit of the sky;
Converse with stars above, and know
All Nature in its forms below;   . 30
The rest it seeks in seeking dies,
And doubts at last for knowledge rise.

   Lovely lasting Peace! appear;
This world itself, if thou art here,
Is once again with Eden blest,   35
And man contains it in his breast.

   'Twas thus, as under shade I stood,
I sung my wishes to the wood,
And, lost in thought, no more perceiv'd
The branches whisper as they wav'd: 40
It seem'd as all the quiet place
Confess'd the presence of the Grace:
When thus she spoke——" Go rule thy will,
" Bid thy wild passions all be still;
" Know God—and bring thy heart to know   45
" The joys which from religion flow;
" Then ev'ry Grace shall prove its guest,
" And I'll be there to crown the rest."

   Oh! by yonder mossy seat,
In my hours of sweet retreat,   50

Might I thus my foul employ
With fenfe of gratitude and joy,
Rais'd, as ancient prophets were,
In heav'nly vifion, praife, and pray'r,
Pleafing all men, hurting none,   55
Pleas'd and blefs'd with God alone;
Then while the gardens take my fight
With all the colours of delight,
While filver waters glide along,
To pleafe my ear and court my fong,   60
I'll lift my voice and tune my ftring,
And thee, great Source of Nature! fing.

   The fun that walks his airy way
To light the world and give the day,
The moon that fhines with borrow'd light,   65
The ftars that gild the gloomy night,
The feas that roll unnumber'd waves,
The wood that fpreads its fhady leaves,
The field whofe ears conceal the grain,
The yellow treafure of the plain;   70
All of thefe, and all I fee,
Should be fung, and fung by me;
They fpeak their Maker as they can,
But want and afk the tongue of man.

   Go fearch among your idle dreams,   75
Your bufy or your vain extremes,
And find a life of equal blifs,
Or own the next begun in this.   78

A HYMN FOR MORNING.

SEE, the ſtar that leads the day
Riſing ſhoots a golden ray,
To make the ſhades of darkneſs go
From heav'n above and earth below,
And warn us early with the ſight
To leave the beds of ſilent night,
From an heart ſincere and ſound,
From its very deepeſt ground,
Send Devotion up on high,
Wing'd with heat, to reach the ſky.
See the time for ſleep has run,
Riſe before or with the ſun,
Lift thine hands, and humbly pray
The Fountain of eternal day,
That as the light ſerenely fair
Illuſtrates all the tracts of air,
The ſacred Spirit ſo may reſt
With quick'ning beams upon thy breaſt,
And kindly clean it all within
From darker blemiſhes of ſin,
And ſhine with grace, until we view
The realm it gilds with glory too.
See the day that dawns in air,
Brings along its toil and care,
From the lap of Night it ſprings
With heaps of bus'neſs on its wings;

Prepare to meet them in a mind
That bows fubmiffively refign'd,
That would to works appointed fall,
And knows that God has order'd all.   30
And whether with a fmall repaft
We break the fober morning faft,
Or in our thoughts and houfes lay
The future methods of the day,
Or early walk abroad to meet   35
Our bus'nefs, with induftrious feet,
Whate'er we think, whate'er we do,
His glory ftill be kept in view.
O Giver of eternal blifs!
Heav'nly Father! grant me this,   40
Grant it all as well as me,
All whofe hearts are fix'd on thee,
Who revere thy Son above,
Who thy facred Spirit love.   44

A HYMN FOR NOON.

THE fun is fwiftly mounted high,
It glitters in the fouthern fky,
Its beams with force and glory beat,
And fruitful earth is fill'd with heat.
Father! alfo with thy fire   5
Warm the cold the dead defire,

And make the sacred love of thee
Within my soul a sun to me:
Let it shine so fairly bright,
That nothing else be took for light,   10
That worldly charms be seen to fade,
And in its lustre find a shade:
Let it strongly shine within,
To scatter all the clouds of sin,
That drive when gusts of passion rise,   15
And intercept it from our eyes:
Let its glory more than vie
With the sun that lights the sky:
Let it swiftly mount in air,
Mount with that, and leave it there,   20
And soar with more aspiring flight
To realms of everlasting light.
Thus, while here I'm forc'd to be,
I daily wish to live with thee,
And feel that union which thy love   25
Will, after death, complete above.
From my soul I send my pray'r,
Great Creator! bow thine ear;
Thou, for whose propitious sway
The world was taught to see the day,   30
Who spake the word, and earth begun,
And shew'd its beauties in the sun,
With pleasure I thy creatures view,
And would with good affection too,

Good affection sweetly free, 35
Loose from them, and move to thee:
O teach me due returns to give,
And to thy glory let me live!
And then my days shall shine the more,
Or pass more blessed than before. 40

A HYMN FOR EVENING.

The beam-repelling mists arise,
And ev'ning spreads obscurer skies:
The twilight will the night forerun,
And night itself be soon begun.
Upon thy knees devoutly bow 5
And pray the Lord of glory now
To fill thy breast, or deadly sin
May cause a blinder night within.
And whether pleasing vapours rise,
Which gently dim the closing eyes, 10
Which makes the weary members blest
With sweet refreshment in their rest,
Or whether spirits in the brain
Dispel their soft embrace again,
And on my watchful bed I stay, 15
Forsook by sleep, and waiting day;
Be God for ever in my view,
And never he forsake me too;

But ſtill as day concludes in night,
To break again with new-born light,   20
His wondrous bounty let me find
With ſtill a more enlighten'd mind.
When grace and love in one agree,
Grace from God, and love from me,
Grace that will from heav'n inſpire,   25
Love that ſeals it in deſire,
Grace and love that mingle beams,
And fill me with increaſing flames.
Thou that haſt thy palace far
Above the moon and every ſtar,   30
Thou that ſitteſt on a throne
To which the night was never known,
Regard my voice, and make me bleſt,
By kindly granting its requeſt.
If thoughts on thee my ſoul employ,   35
My darkneſs will afford me joy,
Till thou ſhalt call and I ſhall ſoar,
And part with darkneſs evermore.   38

TO MR. POPE.

To praife, yet ftill with due refpect to praife,
A bard triumphant in immortal bays;
The learn'd to fhow, the fenfible commend,
Yet ftill preferve the province of the friend;
What life, what vigour, muft the lines require?   5
What mufic tune them? what affection fire?
  O might thy genius in my bofom fhine!
Thou fhouldft not fail of numbers worthy thine;
The brighteft Ancients might at once agree
To fing within my lays, and fing of thee.   10
    Horace himfelf would own thou doft excel
In candid arts to play the critic well;
Ovid himfelf might wifh to fing the dame
Whom Windfor Foreft fees a gliding ftream;
On filver feet, with annual ofier crown'd,   15
She runs for ever thro' poetic ground.
    How flame the glories of Belinda's hair!
Made by thy Mufe the envy of the fair;
Lefs fhone the treffes Egypt's princefs wore,
Which fweet Callimachus fo fung before.   20
Here courtly trifles fet the world at odds,
Belles war with beaux, and whims defcend for gods.
The new machines, in names of ridicule,
Mock the grave frenzy of the chimic fool:

But know, ye Fair! a point conceal'd with art,   25
The Sylphs and Gnomes are but a woman's heart:
The Graces ſtand in ſight; a Satyr train
Peep o'er their heads, and laugh behind the ſcene.
     In Fame's fair temple, o'er the boldeſt wits,
Enſhrin'd on high the ſacred Virgil ſits,   30
And ſits in meaſures ſuch as Virgil's Muſe,
To place thee near him, might be fond to chuſe:
How might he tune th' alternate reed with thee,
Perhaps a Strephon thou, a Daphnis he,
While ſome old Damon, o'er the vulgar wiſe,   35
Thinks he deſerves, and thou deſerv'ſt the prize?
Rapt with the thought, my fancy ſeeks the plains,
And turns me ſhepherd while I hear the ſtrains.
Indulgent nurſe of ev'ry tender gale,
Parent of flowrets, old Arcadia! hail: 40
Here in the cool my limbs at eaſe I ſpread,
Here let thy poplars whiſper o'er my head;
Still ſlide thy waters ſoft among the trees,
Thy aſpins quiver in a breathing breeze;
Smile all thy vallies in eternal ſpring;   45
Be huſh'd, ye Winds! while Pope and Virgil ſing.
     In Engliſh lays, and all ſublimely great,
Thy Homer warms with all his ancient heat;
He ſhines in council, thunders in the fight,
And flames with ev'ry ſenſe of great delight.   50
Long has that poet reign'd, and long unknown,
Like monarchs ſparkling on a diſtant throne;

2

In all the majesty of Greek retir'd,
Himself unknown, his mighty name admir'd,
His language failing wrapp'd him round with night,
Thine, rais'd by thee, recalls the work to light. 56
So wealthy mines, that ages long before
Fed the large realms around with golden ore,
When chok'd by sinking banks, no more appear,
And shepherds only say, " The mines were here;"60
Should some rich youth (if Nature warm his heart,
And all his projects stand inform'd with art)
Here clear the caves, there ope the leading vein,
The mines detected flame with gold again.

    How vast, how copious, are thy new designs! 65
How ev'ry music varies in thy lines!
Still as I read I feel my bosom beat, ,
And rise in raptures by another's heat.
Thus in the wood, when summer dress'd the days,
When Windsor lent us tuneful hours of ease, 70
Our ears the lark, the thrush, the turtle, blest,
And Philomela sweetest o'er the rest;
The shades resound with song—O softly tread!
While a whole season warbles round my head.

    This to my friend—and when a friend inspires, 75
My silent harp its master's hand requires,
Shakes off the dust, and makes these rocks resound,
For Fortune plac'd me in unfertile ground,
Far from the joys that with my soul agree,
From wit, from learning,—far, oh far! from thee, 80

                          E ij

Here moſs-grown trees expand the ſmalleſt leaf,
Here half an acre's corn is half a ſheaf;
Here hills with naked heads the tempeſt meet,
Rocks at their ſide, and torrents at their feet,
Or lazy lakes, unconſcious of a flood,   85
Whoſe dull brown Naiads ever ſleep in mud.

  Yet here Content can dwell, and learned Eaſe,
A friend delight me, and an author pleaſe;
Ev'n here I ſing, while Pope ſupplies the theme
Show my own love, tho' not increaſe his fame.   90

TO A YOUNG LADY,

On her tranſlation of the ſtory of

PHOEBUS AND DAPHNE, FROM OVID.

In Phœbus Wit (as Ovid ſaid)
Enchanting Beauty woo'd;
In Daphne Beauty coily fled,
While vainly Wit purſu'd.

But when you trace what Ovid writ,   5
A diff'rent turn we view;
Beauty no longer flies from Wit,
Since both are join'd in you.

Your lines the wondrous change impart
From whence our laurels fpring,   10
In numbers fram'd to pleafe the heart,
And merit what they fing.

Methinks thy Poet's gentle fhade
Its wreath prefents to thee;
What Daphne owes you as a maid,
She pays you as a tree.   16

E iij

MISCELLANIES.

HESIOD:

OR,

THE RISE OF WOMAN.

Wʜᴀᴛ ancient times (thofe times we fancy wife)
Have left on long record of Woman's rife,
What morals teach it, and what fables hide,
What author wrote it, how that author dy'd,
All thefe I fing. In Greece they fram'd the tale, 5
(In Greece 'twas thought a Woman might be frail.)
Ye modern Beauties! where the poet drew
His fofteft pencil, think he dream'd of you;
And warn'd by him, ye wanton Pens! beware
How Heav'n's concern'd to vindicate the fair. 10
The cafe was Hefiod's; he the fable writ;
Some think with meaning, fome with idle wit:
Perhaps 'tis either, as the ladies pleafe;
I wave the conteft, and commence the lays.

   In days of yore, (no matter where or when, 15
'Twas ere the low creation fwarm'd with men)
That one Prometheus, fprung of heav'nly birth,
(Our author's fong can witnefs) liv'd on earth:

He carv'd the turf to mould a manly frame,
And stole from Jove his animating flame;   20
The fly contrivance o'er Olympus ran,
When thus the monarch of the stars began.
　　" Oh vers'd in arts ! whose daring thoughts aspire
" To kindle clay with never-dying fire !
" Enjoy thy glory past, that gift was thine;   25
" The next thy creature meets be fairly mine :
" And such a gift, a vengeance so defign'd,
" As fuits the counsel of a god to find;
" A pleafing bosom-cheat, a specious ill,
" Which felt they curfe, yet covet still to feel."   30
　　He said, and Vulcan straight the fire commands
To temper mortar with ethereal hands ;
In such a shape to mould a rifing fair,
As virgin-goddeffes are proud to wear;
To make her eyes with diamond-water shine,   35
And form her organs for a voice divine.
'Twas thus the fire ordain'd ; the pow'r obey'd,
And work'd, and wonder'd at the work he made;
The faireft, fofteft, fweeteft, frame beneath,
Now made to feem, now more than feem, to breathe!
　　As Vulcan ends the cheerful queen of charms   41
Clafp'd the new-panting creature in her arms;
From that embrace a fine complexion fpread,
Where mingled whitenefs glow'd with fofter red ;
Then in a kifs she breath'd her various arts   45
Of trifling prettily with wounded hearts;

A mind for love, but still a changing mind,
The lisp affected, and the glance design'd;
The sweet confusing blush, the secret wink,
The gentle-swimming walk, the courteous sink;   50
The stare for strangeness fit, for scorn the frown,
For decent yielding, looks declining down;
The practis'd languish, where well-feign'd desire
Would own its melting in a mutual fire;
Gay smiles to comfort, April show'rs to move,   55
And all the nature, all the art, of love.

   Gold-sceptred Juno next exalts the fair,
Her touch endows her with imperious air,
Self-valuing fancy, highly-crested pride,
Strong sov'reign will, and some desire to chide;   60
For which an eloquence that aims to vex,
With native tropes of anger arms the sex.

   Minerva (skilful goddess) train'd the maid
To twirl the spindle by the twisting thread,
To fix the loom, instruct the reeds to part,   65
Cross the long weft, and close the web with art;
An useful gift; but what profuse expense,
What world of fashions, took its rise from hence!

   Young Hermes next, a close-contriving god,
Her brows encircled with his serpent rod;   70
Then plots and fair excuses fill'd her brain,
The views of breaking am'rous vows for gain,
The price of favours, the designing arts
That aim at riches in contempt of hearts;

And for a comfort in the marriage life, 75
The little pilf'ring temper of a wife.

    Full on the fair his beams Apollo flung,
And fond perfuafion tipp'd her eafy tongue;
He gave her words where oily flatt'ry lays
The pleafing colours of the art of praife; 80
And wit, to fcandal exquifitely prone,
Which frets another's fpleen to cure its own.

    Thofe facred virgins whom the bards revere,
Tun'd all her voice, and fhed a fweetnefs there,
To make her fenfe with double charms abound, 85
Or make her lively nonfenfe pleafe by found.

    To drefs the maid, the decent Graces brought
A robe in all the dies of beauty wrought,
And plac'd their boxes o'er a rich brocade,
Where pictur'd Loves on ev'ry cover play'd; 90
Then fpread thofe implements that Vulcan's art
Had fram'd to merit Cytherea's heart;
The wire to curl, the clofe-indented comb,
To call the locks that lightly wander home,
And, chief, the mirrour, where the ravifh'd maid 95
Beholds and loves her own reflected fhade.

    Fair Flora lent her flores, the purpled Hours
Confin'd her treffes with a wreath of flow'rs;
Within the wreath arofe a radiant crown,
A veil pellucid hung depending down; 100
Back roll'd her azure veil with ferpent fold,
The purfled border deck'd the floor with gold.

Her robe (which clofely by the girdle brac'd
Reveal'd the beauties of a flender wafte)
Flow'd to the feet, to copy Venus' air,   105
When Venus' ftatues have a robe to wear.

  The new-fprung creature, finifh'd thus for harms,
Adjufts her habit, practifes her charms,
With blufhes glows, or fhines with lively fmiles,
Confirms her will, or recollects her wiles: 110
Then confcious of her worth, with eafy pace
Glides by the glafs, and turning views her face.

  A finer flax than what they wrought before,
Thro' Time's deep cave the Sifter Fates explore,
Then fix the loom, their fingers nimbly weave,   115
And thus their toil prophetic fongs deceive.

  " Flow from the rock, my Flax! and fwiftly flow,
" Purfue thy thread, the fpindle runs below:
" A creature fond and changing, fair and vain,
" The creature Woman, rifes now to reign: 120
" New beauty blooms, a beauty form'd to fly;
" New love begins, a love produc'd to die;
" New parts diftrefs the troubled fcenes of life,
" The fondling miftrefs and the ruling wife.

  " Men, born to labour, all with pains provide, 125
" Women have time to facrifice to pride;
" They want the care of man, their want they know,
" And drefs to pleafe with heart-alluring fhow;
" The fhow prevailing, for the fway contend,
" And make a fervant where they meet a friend. 130

" Thus in a thoufand wax-erected forts
" A loitering race the painful bee fupports;
" From fun to fun, from bank to bank, he flies,
" With honey loads his bag, with wax his thighs;
" Fly where he will, at home the race remain,   135
" Prune the filk drefs, and murm'ring eat the gain.

  " Yet here and there we grant a gentle bride,
" Whofe temper betters by the father's fide;
" Unlike the reft that double human care,
" Fond to relieve, or refolute to fhare: 140
" Happy the man whom thus his ftars advance!
" The curfe is gen'ral, but the blefling chance."

  Thus fung the Sifters, while the gods admire
Their beauteous creature, made for man in ire;
The young Pandora fhe, whom all contend   145
To make too perfect not to gain her end;
Then bid the winds that fly to breathe the fpring
Return to bear her on a gentle wing:
With wafting airs the winds obfequious blow,
And land the fhining vengeance fafe below: 150
A golden coffer in her hand fhe bore,
(The prefent treach'rous, but the bearer more)
'Twas fraught with pangs, for Jove ordain'd above
That gold fhould aid, and pangs attend on Love.

  Her gay defcent the man perceiv'd afar,   155
Wond'ring, he run to catch the falling ftar;
But fo furpris'd, as none but he can tell,
Who lov'd fo quickly, and who lov'd fo well!

O'er all his veins the wand'ring passion burns,
He calls her Nymph, and ev'ry nymph by turns: 160
Her form to lovely Venus' he prefers,
Or swears that Venus' must be such as her's.
She, proud to rule, yet strangely fram'd to teize,
Neglects his offers while her airs she plays,
Shoots scornful glances from the bended frown, 165
In brisk disorder trips it up and down,
Then hums a careless tune to lay the storm,
And sits and blushes, smiles, and yields in form.

  " Now take, what Jove design'd, (she softly cry'd)
" This box thy portion, and myself thy bride." 170
Fir'd with the prospect of the double charms,
He snatch'd the box and bride with eager arms.

  Unhappy man! to whom so bright she shone,
The fatal gift, her tempting self, unknown!
The winds were silent, all the waves asleep, 175
And heav'n was trac'd upon the flatt'ring deep;
But whilst he looks, unmindful of a storm,
And thinks the water wears a stable form,
What dreadful din around his ears shall rise!
What frowns confuse his picture of the skies! 180
  At first the creature man was fram'd alone
Lord of himself, and all the world his own;
For him the Nymphs in green forsook the woods,
For him the Nymphs in blue forsook the floods;
In vain the Satyrs rage, the Tritons rave, 185
They bore him heroes in the secret cave;

3

No care deftroy'd, no fick diforder prey'd,
No bending age his fprightly form decay'd;
No wars were known, no females beard to rage,
And poets tell us 'twas a Golden Age.   190
    When Woman came, thefe ills the box confin'd
Burft furious out, and poifon'd all the wind;
From point to point, from pole to pole, they flew,
Spread as they went, and in the progrefs grew:
The Nymphs regretting left the mortal race,   195
And alt'ring Nature wore a fickly face:
New terms of folly rofe, new ftates of care,
New plagues, to fuffer and to pleafe the fair!
The days of whining and of wild intrigues
Commenc'd, or finifh'd with the breach of leagues;
The mean defigns of well-diffembled love,   201
The fordid matches never join'd above;
Abroad the labour, and at home the noife,
(Man's double fuff'rings for domeftic joys)
The curfe of jealoufy, expenfe and ftrife,   205
Divorce, the publick brand of fhameful life;
The rival's fword, the qualm that takes the fair,
Difdain for paffion, paffion in defpair——
Thefe, and a thoufand yet unnam'd, we find;
Ah, fear the thoufand yet unnam'd behind!   210
    Thus on Parnaffus tuneful Hefiod fung,
The mountain echo'd, and the valley rung,
The facred groves a fix'd attention fhow,
The cryftal Helicon forbore to flow,

The fky grew bright, and (if his verfe be true) 215
The Mufes came to give the laurel too.
But what avail'd the verdant prize of wit,
If Love fwore vengeance for the tales he writ?
Ye Fair offended! hear your friend relate
What heavy judgment prov'd the writer's fate, 220
Tho' when it happen'd no relation clears,
'Tis thought in five, or five-and-twenty years.

    Where, dark and filent, with a twifted fhade
The neighb'ring woods a native arbour made,
There oft a tender pair for am'rous play 225
Retiring, toy'd the ravifh'd hours away ;
A Locrian youth, the gentle Troilus he,
A fair Milefian, kind Evanthe fhe ;
But fwelling Nature in a fatal hour
Betray'd the fecrets of the confcious bow'r ; 230
The dire difgrace her brothers count their own,
And track her fteps to make its author known.

    It chanc'd one ev'ning, ('twas the lovers' day)
Conceal'd in brakes the jealous kindred lay,
When Hefiod wand'ring, mus'd along the plain, 235
And fix'd his feat where Love had fix'd the fcene : .
A ftrong fufpicion ftraight poffeft their mind,
(For poets ever were a gentle kind)
But when Evanthe near the paffage ftood,
Flung back a doubtful look, and fhot the wood: 240
" Now take (at once they cry) thy due reward,"
And, urg'd with erring rage, affault the bard.

His corpfe the fea receiv'd. The dolphins bore
('Twas all the gods would do) the corpfe to fhore.
 Methinks I view the dead with pitying eyes, 245
And fee the dreams of ancient Wifdom rife;
I fee the Mufes round the body cry,
But hear a Cupid loudly laughing by;
He wheels his arrow with infulting hand,
And thus infcribes the moral on the fand; 250
" Here Hefiod lies: ye future Bards! beware
" How far your moral tales incenfe the fair:
" Unlov'd, unloving, 'twas his fate to bleed;
" Without his quiver Cupid caus'd the deed:
" He judg'd this turn of malice juftly due,
" And Hefiod dy'd for joys he never knew. 256

THE HERMIT.

Far in a wild, unknown to public view,
From youth to age a rev'rend Hermit grew;
The mofs his bed, the cave his humble cell,
His food the fruits, his drink the cryftal well;
Remote from man, with God he pafs'd the days,   5
Pray'r all his bus'nefs, all his pleafure praife.

  A life fo facred, fuch ferene repofe,
Seem'd heav'n itfelf, till one fuggeftion rofe,
That Vice fhould triumph, Virtue Vice obey;
This fprung fome doubt of Providence's fway: 10
His hopes no more a certain profpect boaft,
And all the tenour of his foul is loft:
So when a fmooth expanfe receives impreft
Calm Nature's image on its watry breaft,
Down bend the banks, the trees depending grow,
And fkies beneath with anfw'ring colours glow;   16
But if a ftone the gentle fea divide,
Swift ruffling circles curl on ev'ry fide,
And glimmering fragments of a broken fun,
Banks, trees, and fkies, in thick diforder run.   20

  To clear this doubt, to know the world by fight,
To find if books or fwains report it right,
(For yet by fwains alone the world he knew,
Whofe feet came wand'ring o'er the nightly dew)
He quits his cell: the pilgrim-ftaff he bore,   25
And fix'd the fcallop in his hat before;

Then with the sun a rising journey went,
Sedate to think, and watching each event.

    The morn was wasted in the pathless grass,
And long and lonesome was the wild to pass;   30
But when the southern sun had warm'd the day,
A youth came posting o'er a crossing way;
His raiment decent, his complexion fair,
And soft in graceful ringlets wav'd his hair:
Then near approaching, "Father! hail," he cry'd; 35
And, "Hail, my Son!" the rev'rend Sire reply'd;
Words follow'd words, from question answer flow'd,
And talk of various kind deceiv'd the road;
Till each with other pleas'd, and loath to part,
While in their age they differ, join in heart: 40
Thus stands an aged elm in ivy bound,
Thus youthful ivy clasps an elm around.

    Now sunk the sun; the closing hour of day
Came onward, mantled o'er with sober gray;
Nature in silence bid the world repose;   45
When near the road a stately palace rose:
There by the moon thro' ranks of trees they pass,
Whose verdure crown'd their sloping sides of grass.
It chanc'd the noble master of the dome
Still made his house the wand'ring stranger's home;
Yet still the kindness, from a thirst of praise,   51
Prov'd the vain flourish of expensive ease.
The pair arrive; the liv'ry'd servants wait;
Their lord receives them at the pompous gate.

The table groans with coſtly piles of food,   55
And all is more than hoſpitably good.
Then led to reſt, the day's long toil they drown,
Deep ſunk in ſleep, and ſilk, and heaps of down.
　　At length 'tis morn, and at the dawn of day
Along the wide canals the Zephyrs play ;   60
Freſh o'er the gay parterres the breezes creep,
And ſhake the neighb'ring wood to baniſh ſleep.
Up riſe the gueſts, obedient to the call;
An early banquet deck'd the ſplendid hall ;
Rich luſcious wine a golden goblet grac'd,   65
Which the kind maſter forc'd the gueſts to taſte.
Then pleas'd and thankful, from the porch they go,
And but the landlord none had cauſe of woe :
His cup was vaniſh'd; for in ſecret guiſe
The younger gueſt purloin'd the glittering prize. 70
　　As one who ſpies a ſerpent in his way,
Gliſt'ning and baſking in the ſummer-ray,
Diſorder'd ſtops to ſhun the danger near,
Then walks with faintneſs on, and looks with fear;
So ſeem'd the Sire, when far upon the road   75
The ſhining ſpoil his wily partner ſhow'd.
He ſtopp'd with ſilence, walk'd with trembling heart,
And much he wiſh'd, but durſt not aſk to part :
Murm'ring he lifts his eyes, and thinks it hard
That generous actions meet a baſe reward.   80
　　While thus they paſs, the ſun his glory ſhrouds,
The changing ſkies hang out their ſable clouds ;

A found in air prefag'd approaching rain,
And beafts to covert fkud acrofs the plain.
Warn'd by the figns, the wand'ring pair retreat, 85
To feek for fhelter at a neighb'ring feat.
'Twas built with turrets, on a rifing ground,
And ftrong, and large, and unimprov'd around;
Its owner's temper tim'rous and fevere,
Unkind and griping, caus'd a defert there. 90
As near the mifer's heavy doors they drew,
Fierce rifing gufts with fudden fury blew;
The nimble lightning mix'd with fhow'rs began,
And o'er their heads loud-rolling thunder ran.
Here long they knock, but knock or call in vain, 95
Driv'n by the wind, and batter'd by the rain.
At length fome pity warm'd the mafter's breaft;
('Twas then his threfhold firft receiv'd a gueft)
Slow creaking turns the door with jealous care,
And half he welcomes in the fhivering pair; . 100
One frugal faggot lights the naked walls,
And Nature's fervour thro' their limbs recalls:
Bread of the coarfeft fort, with eager wine,
(Each hardly granted) ferv'd them both to dine;
And when the tempeft firft appear'd to ceafe, 105
A ready warning bid them part in peace.
      With ftill remark the pond'ring Hermit view'd
In one fo rich a life fo poor and rude;
And why fhould fuch, (within himfelf he cry'd)
Lock the loft wealth a thoufand want befide? 110

But what new marks of wonder foon took place
In every fettling feature of his face,
When from his veft the young companion bore
That cup the gen'rous landlord own'd before,
And paid profufely with the precious bowl   115
The ftinted kindnefs of this churlifh foul !

But now the clouds in airy tumult fly,
The fun emerging opes an azure fky;
A frefher green the fmelling leaves difplay,
And, glitt'ring as they tremble, cheer the day : 120
The weather courts them from the poor retreat,
And the glad mafter bolts the wary gate.

While hence they walk, the pilgrim's bofom wrought
With all the travel of uncertain thought;
His partner's acts without their caufe appear,   125
'Twas there a vice, and feem'd a madnefs here :
Detefting that, and pitying this, he goes,
Loft and confounded with the various fhows.

Now night's dim fhades again involve the fky;
Again the wand'rers want a place to lie;   130
Again they fearch, and find a lodging nigh :
The foil improv'd around, the manfion neat,
And neither poorly low nor idly great,
It feem'd to fpeak its mafter's turn of mind,
Content, and not for praife but virtue kind.   135

Hither the walkers turn with weary feet,
Then blefs the manfion, and the mafter greet :

Their greeting fair, bestow'd with modest guise,
The courteous master hears, and thus replies:
  " Without a vain, without a grudging heart,   140
" To him who gives us all I yield a part;
" From him you come, for him accept it here,
" A frank and sober, more than costly, cheer."
He spoke, and bid the welcome table spread,
Then talk'd of virtue till the time of bed,   145
When the grave houshold round his hall repair,
Warn'd by a bell, and close the hours with pray'r.
  At length the world, renew'd by calm repose,
Was strong for toil, the dappled Morn arose;
Before the pilgrims part the younger crept   150
Near the clos'd cradle where an infant slept,
And writh'd his neck: the landlord's little pride,
O strange return! grew black, and gasp'd, and dy'd.
Horror of horrors! what! his only son!
How look'd our Hermit when the fact was done? 155
Not hell, tho' hell's black jaws in sunder part,
And breathe blue fire, could more assault his heart.
  Confus'd, and struck with silence at the deed,
He flies, but, trembling, fails to fly with speed.
His steps the youth pursues; the country lay   160
Perplex'd with roads; a servant show'd the way:
A river cross'd the path; the passage o'er
Was nice to find; the servant trod before:
Long arms of oaks an open bridge supply'd,
And deep the waves beneath the bending glide. 165

The youth, who feem'd to watch a time to fin,
Approach'd the carelefs guide, and thruft him in;
Plunging he falls, and rifing lifts his head,
Then flafhing turns, and finks among the dead!

Wild, fparkling rage inflames the Father's eyes,
He burfts the bands of fear, and madly cries,   171
" Detefted Wretch!"——But fcarce his fpeech began,
When the ftrange partner feem'd no longer man:
His youthful face grew more ferenely fweet; ·
His robe turn'd white, and flow'd upon his feet; 175
Fair rounds of radiant points inveft his hair;   · . .
Celeftial odours breathe thro' purpled air;   . .
And wings, whofe colours glitter'd on the day,
Wide at his back their gradual plumes difplay. -
The form ethereal burfts upon his fight,   180
And moves in all the majefty of light.   ~

Tho' loud at firft the pilgrim's paffion grew,
Sudden he gaz'd, and wift not what to do; ·
Surprife in fecret chains his words fufpends,   ·
And in a calm his fettling temper ends.   185
But filence here the beauteous angel broke,
(The voice of mufic ravifh'd as he fpoke.)

" Thy pray'r, thy praife, thy life, to vice unknown,
" In fweet memorial rife before the throne:
" Thefe charms fuccefs in our bright region find, 190
" And force an angel down to calm thy mind;
" For this commiffion'd, I forfook the fky:
" Nay, ceafe to kneel——thy fellow-fervant I.

" Then know the truth of government divine,
" And let these scruples be no longer thine.   195
   " The Maker justly claims that world he made,
" In this the right of Providence is laid;
" Its sacred majesty thro' all depends
" On using second means to work his ends:
" 'Tis thus, withdrawn in state from human eye, 200
" The pow'r exerts his attributes on high,
" Your actions uses, nor controuls your will,
" And bids the doubting sons of men be still.
   " What strange events can strike with more surprise
" Than those which lately strook thy wond'ring eyes?
" Yet taught by these, confess th' Almighty just, 206
" And where you can't unriddle learn to trust.
   " The great vain man who far'd on costly food,
" Whose life was too luxurious to be good,
" Who made his iv'ry stands with goblets shine, 210
" And forc'd his guests to morning draughts of wine,
" Has with the cup the graceless custom lost,
" And still he welcomes, but with less of cost.
   " The mean suspicious wretch, whose bolted door
" Ne'er mov'd in duty to the wand'ring poor, 215
" With him I left the cup, to teach his mind
" That Heav'n can bless if mortals will be kind.
" Conscious of wanting worth, he views the bowl,
" And feels compassion touch his grateful soul.
" Thus artists melt the sullen ore of lead,   220
" With heaping coals of fire upon its head;

" In the kind warmth the metal learns to glow,
" And loose from drofs the filver runs below.
   " Long had our pious friend in virtue trod,
" But now the child half-wean'd his heart from God;
" (Child of his age) for him he liv'd in pain,   226
" And meafur'd back his fteps to earth again.
" To what exceffes had his dotage run!
" But God to fave the father took the fon.
" To all but thee in fits he feem'd to go,   230
" (And 'twas my miniftry to deal the blow.)
" The poor fond parent, humbled in the duft,
" Now owns in tears the punifhment was juft.
   " But now had all his fortune felt a wrack,
" Had that falfe fervant fped in fafety back: 235
" This night his treafur'd heaps he meant to fteal,
" And what a fund of charity would fail!
   " Thus Heav'n inftructs thy mind: this trial o'er,
" Depart in peace, refign, and fin no more."
On founding pinions here the youth withdrew,
The fage ftood wond'ring as the feraph flew.   241
Thus look'd Elifha, when to mount on high
His mafter took the chariot of the fky;
The fiery pomp afcending left the view;
The prophet gaz'd, and wifh'd to follow too.   245
   The bending Hermit here a pray'r begun,
" Lord! as in heav'n, on earth thy will be done."
Then gladly turning, fought his ancient place,
And pafs'd a life of piety and peace.   249

A FAIRY TALE,

IN THE ANCIENT ENGLISH STYLE.

In Britain's isle and Arthur's days,
When midnight Faeries daunc'd the maze,
Liv'd Edwin of the Green;
Edwin, I wis a gentle youth,
Endow'd with courage, fenfe, and truth,   5
Tho' badly fhap'd he been.

His mountain back mote well be faid
To meafure height againft his head,
And lift it felf above;
Yet fpite of all that Nature did   10
To make his uncouth form forbid,
This creature dar'd to love.

He felt the charms of Edith's eyes,
Nor wanted hope to gain the prize,
Could ladies look within;   15
But one Sir Topaz drefs'd with art,
And, if a fhape could win a heart,
He had a fhape to win.

Edwin (if right I read my fong)
With flighted paffion pac'd along   20
All in the moony light:
'Twas near an old enchaunted court,
Where fportive Faeries made refort
To revel out the night.

His heart was drear, his hope was croft,   25
'Twas late, 'twas farr, the path was loft
That reach'd the neighbour-town:
With weary fteps he quits the fhades,
Refolv'd, the darkling dome he treads,
And drops his limbs adown.   30

But fcant he lays him on the floor,
When hollow winds remove the door,
A trembling rocks the ground;
And (well I ween to count aright)
At once an hundred tapers light   35
On all the walls around.

Now founding tongues affail his ear,
Now founding feet approachen near,
And now the founds encreafe,
And from the corner where he lay   40
He fees a train profufely gay
Come pranckling o'er the place.

But (truſt me, Gentles!) never yet
Was dight a maſquing half ſo neat,
Or half ſo rich before ;   45
The country lent the ſweet perfumes,
The ſea the pearl, the ſky the plumes,
The town its ſilken ſtore.

Now whilſt he gaz'd a gallant, dreſt
In flaunting robes above the reſt,   50
With awfull accent cry'd ;
" What mortall of a wretched mind,
" Whoſe ſighs infect the balmy wind,
" Has here preſum'd to hide ?"

At this the ſwain, whoſe vent'rous ſoul   55
No fears of magic art controul,
Advanc'd in open ſight :
" Nor have I cauſe of dreed," he ſaid,
" Who view (by no preſumption led)
" Your revels of the night.   60

" 'Twas grief, for ſcorn of faithful love,
" Which made my ſteps unweeting rove
" Amid the nightly dew."
" 'Tis well," the gallant cries again ;
" We Faeries never injure men   65
" Who dare to tell us true.

G ij

" Exalt thy love-dejected heart,
" Be mine the tafk, or ere we part,
" To make thee grief refign :
" Now take the pleafure of thy chaunce,   70
" Whilft I with Mab, my part'ner, daunce,
" Be little Mable thine."

He fpoke, and all a fudden there
Light mufick flotes in wanton air ;
The monarch leads the Queen :   75
The reft their Faerie partners found,
And Mable trimly tript the ground
With Edwin of the Green.

The dauncing paft, the board was laid,
And fiker fuch a feaft was made   80
As heart and lip defire ;
Withouten hands the difhes fly,
The glaffes with a wifh come nigh,
And with a wifh retire.

But now, to pleafe the Faerie King,   85
Full ev'ry deal they laugh and fing,
And antick feats devife ;
Some wind and tumble like an ape,
And other fome tranfmute their fhape
In Edwin's wond'ring eyes :   90

Till one, at last, that Robin hight,
(Renown'd for pinching maids by night)
Has hent him up aloof;
And full against the beam he flung,
Where by the back the youth he hung   95
To spraul unneath the roof.

From thence, " Reverse my charm," he crys,
" And let it fairly now suffice
" The gambol has been shown."
But Oberon answers with a smile,   100
" Content thee, Edwin, for a while,
" The vantage is thine own."

Here ended all the phantome play,
They smelt the fresh approach of day,
And heard a cock to crow;   105
The whirling wind that bore the crowd
Has clapp'd the door, and whistled loud,
To warn them all to go.

Then screaming all at once they fly,
And all at once the tapers dy;   110
Poor Edwin falls to floor:
Forlorn his state, and dark the place,
Was never wight in sicke a case
Through all the land before.

But foon as Dan Apollo rofe,   115
Full jolly creature home he goes,
He feels his back the lefs;
His honeft tongue and fteady mind
Han ride him of the lump behind
Which made him want fuccefs.   120

With lufty livelyhed he talks,
He feems a-dauncing as he walks;
His ftory foon took wind;
And beauteous Edith fees the youth
Endow'd with courage, fenfe, and truth,   125
Without a bunch behind.

The ftory told, Sir Topaz mov'd,
(The youth of Edith erft approv'd)
To fee the revel fcene:
At clofe of eve he leaves his home,   130
And wends to find the ruin'd dome
All on the gloomy plain.

As there he bides, it fo befell,
The wind came ruftling down a dell,
A fhaking feiz'd the wall: 135
Up fpring the tapers as before,
The Faeries bragly foot the floor,
And mufick fills the hall.

But certes, forely funk with woe,
Sir Topaz fees the Elfin fhow,   140
His fpirits in him dy;
When Oberon cries, " A man is near,
" A mortall paffion, cleeped Fear,
" Hangs flagging in the fky."

With that Sir Topaz (haplefs youth !)   145
In accents fault'ring, ay for ruth
Intreats them pity graunt;
For als he been a mifter wight
Betray'd by wand'ring in the night
To tread the circled haunt.   150

" Ah, Lofell vile !" at once they roar,
" And little fkill'd of Faerie lore,
" Thy caufe to come we know:
" Now bas thy keftrell courage fell,
" And Faeries, fince a ly you tell,   155
" Are free to work thee woe."

Then Will, who bears the wifpy fire
To trail the fwains among the mire,
The caitive upward flung;
There like a tortoife in a fhop   160
He dangled from the chamber-top,
Where whilome Edwin hung.

The revel now proceeds apace,
Deffly they frifk it o'er the place,
They fit, they drink, and eat;   165
The time with frolick mirth beguile,
And poor Sir Topaz hangs·the while
Till all the rout retreat.

By this the ftarrs began to wink,
They fkriek, they fly, the tapers fink,   170
And down ydrops the knight;
For never fpell by Faerie laid
With ftrong enchantment bound a glade
Beyond the length of night.

Chill, dark, alone, adreed, he lay,   175
Till up the welkin rofe the day,
Then deem'd the dole was o'er:
But wot ye well his harder lot?
His feely back the bunch has got
Which Edwin loft afore.   180

This tale a Sybil-nurfe ared;
She foftly ftrok'd my youngling head,
And when the tale was done,
"Thus fome are born, my Son, (fhe cries)
"With bafe impediments to rife,   185
"And fome are born with none.

" But Virtue can it felf advance
" To what the fav'rite fools of Chance
" By Fortune feem'd defign'd ;
" Virtue can gain the odds of Fate,   190
" And from it felf fhake off the weight
" Upon th' unworthy mind."   192

THE VIGIL OF VENUS.

Written in the time of Julius Cæsar, and by some ascribed to Catullus.

" Let those love now who never lov'd before;
" Let those who always lov'd now love the more."
The spring, the new, the warb'ling spring, appears,
The youthful season of reviving years.
In spring the Loves enkindle mutual heats,   5
The feather'd nation chuse their tuneful mates,
The trees grow fruitful with descending rain,
And dress'd in diff'ring greens adorn the plain.
She comes; to-morrow Beauty's Empress roves
Thro' walks that winding run within the groves; 10
She twines the shooting myrtle into bow'rs,
And ties their meeting tops with wreaths of flow'rs,
Then rais'd sublimely on her easy throne,
From Nature's pow'rful dictates draws her own.

PERVIGILIUM VENERIS.

" Cras amet qui numquam amavit;
" Quique amavit cras amet."
Ver novum, ver jam canorum : vere natus orbis est,
Vere concordant amores, vere nubent alites,
Et nemus comam resolvit de maritis imbribus.
Cras amorem copulatrix inter umbras arborum
Implicat gazas virentes de flagello myrteo.
Cras Dione jura dicit, fulta sublimi throno.

" Let thofe love now who never lov'd before;   15
" Let thofe who always lov'd now love the more."
   'Twas on that day which faw the teeming flood
Swell round, impregnate with celeſtial blood;
Wand'ring in circles ſtood the finny crew,
The midſt was left a void expanfe of blue,   20
There parent Ocean work'd with heaving throes,
And dropping wet the fair Dione rofe.
" Let thofe love now who never lov'd before;
" Let thofe who always lov'd now love the more."
   She paints the purple year with vary'd ſhow,   25
Tips the green gem, and makes the bloſſom glow :
She makes the turgid buds receive the breeze,
Expand to leaves, and ſhade the naked trees :
When gath'ring damps the miſty nights diffuſe,
She fprinkles all the morn with balmy dews;   30

" Cras amet qui numquam amavit ;
" Quique amavit cras amet."
   Tunc liquore de fuperno, fpumeo ponti e globo,
Cærulas inter catervas, inter et bipedes equos,
Fecit undantem Dionen de maritis imbribus.
" Cras amet qui numquam amavit ;
" Quique amavit cras amet."
   Ipfa gemmas purpurantem pingit annum floribus,
Ipfa furgentis papillas de Favoni fpiritu,
Urguet in toros tepentes ; ipfa roris lucidi,
Noctis aura quem relinquit, fpargit umentis aquas,

Bright trembling pearls depend at ev'ry fpray,
And, kept from falling, feem to fall away:
A gloffy frefhnefs hence the rofe receives,
And blufhes fweet through all her filken leaves;
(The drops defcending through the filent night,   35
While ftars ferenely roll their golden light)
Clofe till the morn her humid veil fhe holds, ·
Then deck'd with virgin pomp the flow'r unfolds.
Soon will the morning blufh; ye Maids! prepare,
In rofy garlands bind your flowing hair;   40
'Tis Venus' plant; the blood fair Venus fhed
O'er the gay beauty pour'd immortal red;
From Love's foft kifs a fweet ambrofial fmell
Was taught for ever on the leaves to dwell;
From gems, from flames, from orient rays of light
The richeft luftre makes her purple bright,   46
And fhe to-morrow weds; the fporting gale
Unties her zone, fhe burfts the verdant veil:

Et micant lacrymæ trementes decidivo pondere.
Gutta præceps orbe parvo fuftinet cafus fuos.
In pudorem florulentæ prodiderunt purpuræ.
Umor ille, quem ferenis aftra rorant noctibus.
Mane virgines papillas folvit umenti peplo.
Ipfa juffit mane ut udæ virgines nubant rofæ
Fufæ prius de cruore deque amoris ofculis,
Deque gemmis, deque flammis, deque folis purpuris.

4

Thro' all her sweets the rifling lover flies,
And as he breathes her glowing fires arise.   50
" Let those love now who never lov'd before;
" Let those who always lov'd now love the more."
    Now fair Dione to the myrtle grove
Sends the gay nymphs, and sends her tender Love.
And shall they venture? is it safe to go ?   55
While nymphs have hearts, and Cupid wears a bow?
Yes, safely venture, 'tis his mother's will;
He walks unarm'd, and undesigning ill,
His torch extinct, his quiver useless hung,
His arrows idle, and his bow unstrung :   60
And yet, ye Nymphs! beware, his eyes have charms,
And Love that's naked still is Love in arms.

Cras ruborum qui latebat veste tectus ignea,
Unica marito nodo non pudebit solvere.
" Cras amet qui numquam amavit;
" Quique amavit cras amet."
    Ipsa Nimfas Diva luco jussit ire myrteo
Et puer comes puellis. Nec tamen credi potest
Esse Amorem feriatum, si sagittas vexerit.
Ite Nimfæ : posuit arma, feriatus est Amor.
Jussus est inermis ire, nudus ire jussus est :
Neu quid arcu, neu sagitta, neu quid igne læderet.
Sed tamen cavete Nimfæ, quod Cupido pulcher est :
Totus est inermis idem, quando nudus est amor.

" Let thofe love now who never lov'd before ;
" Let thofe who always lov'd now love the more."
   From Venus' bow'r to Delia's lodge repairs   65
A virgin train, complete with modeft airs :
" Chafte Delia ! grant our fuit ; or fhun the wood,
" Nor ftain this facred lawn with favage blood.
" Venus, O Delia ! if fhe could perfuade,
" Would afk thy prefence, might fhe afk a maid?"70
Here cheerful quires for three aufpicious nights
With fongs prolong the pleafurable rites :
Here crowds in meafures lightly-decent rove,
Oi feek by pairs the covert of the grove,
Where meeting greens for arbours arch above,   75
And mingling flowrets ftrow the fcenes of love :
Here dancing Ceres fhakes her golden fheaves;
Here Bacchus revels, deckt with viny leaves;

" Cras amet qui numquam amavit ;
" Quique amavit cras amet."
   Compari Venus pudore mittit ad te virgines.
Una res eft quam rogamus, cede virgo Delia,
Ut nemus fit incruentum de ferinis ftragibus.
Ipfa vellet ut venires, fi deceret virginem :
Jam tribus choros videres feriatos noctibus :
Congreges inter catervas ire par faltus tuos,
Floreas inter coronas, myrteas inter cafas.
Nec Ceres, nec Bacchus abfunt, nec poetarum Deus ;

Here Wit's enchanting god, in laurel crown'd,
Wakes all the ravifh'd hours with filver found.   80
Ye Fields! ye Forefts! own Dione's reign,
And Delia, huntrefs Delia, fhun the plain.
" Let thofe love now who never lov'd before;
" Let thofe who always lov'd now love the more."
    Gay with the bloom of all her opening year,   85
The queen at Hybla bids her throne appear,
And there prefides ; and there the fav'rite band
(Her fmiling Graces) fhare the great command.
Now, beauteous Hybla! drefs thy flow'ry beds
With all the pride the lavifh feafon fheds ;   90
Now all thy colours, all thy fragrance, yield,
And rival Enna's aromatic field.
To fill the prefence of the gentle court,
From ev'ry quarter rural nymphs refort,

Decinent et tota nox eft pervigila cantibus.
Regnet in filvis Dione : tu recede Delia.
" Cras amet qui numquam amavit ;
" Quique amavit cras amet."
    Juffit Hiblæis tribunal ftare diva floribus.
Præfens ipfa jura dicit, adfederunt Gratiæ.
Hibla totos funde flores quidquid annus adtulit.
Hibla florum rumpe veftem, quantus Ænnæ cam-
       pus eft.
Ruris hic erunt puellæ, vel puellæ montium,

From woods, from mountains, from their humble vales,
From waters curling with the wanton gales.   96
Pleas'd with the joyful train, the laughing queen,
In circles feats them round the bank of green;
And, " Lovely Girls! (fhe whifpers) guard your hearts,
" My boy, tho' ftript of arms, abounds in arts." ·
" Let thofe love now who never lov'd before;   101
" Let thofe who always lov'd now love the more."
    Let tender grafs in fhaded alleys fpread,
Let early flow'rs erect their painted head :
To-morrow's glory be to-morrow feen,   105
That day old Ether wedded Earth in green ;
The Vernal Father bid the fpring appear,
In clouds he coupled to produce the year,
The fap defcending o'er her bofom ran,
And all the various forts of foul began.   110

Quæque filvas, quæque lucos, quæque montes incolunt.
Juffit omnis adfidere pueri mater alitas,
Juffit et nudo puellas nil Amori credere.
" Cras amet qui numquam amavit;
" Quique amavit cras amet."
    Et recentibus virentes ducat umbras floribus.
Cras erat qui primus æther copulavit nuptias,
Ut pater roris crearet vernis annum nubibus
In finum maritus imber fluxit almæ conjugis,
Ut fœtus immixtus omnis aleret magno corpore.

By wheels unknown to fight, by fecret veins
Diftilling life, the fruitful goddefs reigns,
Through all the lovely realms of native day,
Through all the circled land and circling fea,
With fertile feed fhe fill'd the pervious earth,   115
And ever fix'd the myftic ways of birth.
" Let thofe love now who never lov'd before;
" Let thofe who always lov'd now love the more."
   'Twas fhe the parent to the Latian fhore
Through various dangers Troy's remainder bore:
She won Lavinia for her warlike fon,   121
And winning her the Latian empire won:
She gave to Mars the maid whofe honour'd womb
Swell'd with the founder of immortal Rome:
Decoy'd by fhows, the Sabin dames fhe led,   125
And taught our vig'rous youth the means to wed:

Ipfa venas atque mentem permeante fpiritu
Intus occultis gubernat procreatrix viribus,
Perque cœlum, perque terras, perque pontum fubdi-
Pervium fui tenorem feminali tramite   [tum,
Imbuit, juffitque mundum noffe nafcendi vias.
" Cras amet qui numquam amavit;
" Quique amavit cras amet."
   Ipfa Trojanos nepotes in Latino tranftulit;
Ipfa Laurentem puellam conjugem nato dedit:
Moxque Marti de facello dat pudicam virginem.
Romuleas ipfa fecit cum Sabinis nuptias,

Hence fprung the Romans, hence the race divine
Through which great Cæfar draws his Julian line.
" Let thofe love now who never lov'd before;
" Let thofe who always lov'd now love the more."
　　In rural feats the foul of pleafure reigns,　　131
The life of beauty fills the rural fcenes;
Ev'n Love (if Fame the truth of Love declare)
Drew firft the breathings of a rural air.
Some pleafing meadow pregnant Beauty preft,　135
She laid her infant on its flow'ry breaft,
From Nature's fweets he fipp'd the fragrant dew,
He fmil'd, he kifs'd them, and by kiffing grew.
" Let thofe love now who never lov'd before;
" Let thofe who always lov'd now love the more."
　　Now bulls o'er ftalks of broom extend their fides,
Secure of favours from their loving brides:　　142

Unde Ramnes et Quirites, proque prole pofterûm
Romuli matrem crearet et nepotem Cæfarem.
" Cras amet qui numquam amavit;
" Quique amavit cras amet."
　　Rura fœcundat voluptas : rura Venerem fentiunt.
Ipfe Amor puer Dionæ rure natus dicitur.
Hunc ager cum parturiret, ipfa fufcepit finu,
Ipfa florum delicatis educavit ofculis.
" Cras amet qui numquam amavit;
" Quique amavit cras amet."
　　Ecce, jam fuper geniftas explicant tauri latus.

Now ftately rams their fleecy conforts lead,
Who bleating follow thro' the wand'ring fhade ;
And now the goddefs bids the birds appear,   145
Raife all their mufic, and falute the year :
Then deep the fwan begins, and deep the fong
Runs o'er the water where he fails along :
While Philomela tunes a treble ftrain,
And from the poplar charms the lift'ning plain, 150
We fancy love exprefs'd at ev'ry note,
It melts, it warbles, in her liquid throat :
Of barb'rous Tereus fhe complains no more,
But fings for pleafure, as for grief before ;
And ftill her graces rife, her airs extend,   155
And all is filence till the Syren end.

   How long in coming is my lovely Spring !
And when fhall I, and when the fwallow, fing ?
Sweet Philomela ! ceafe,——or here I fit,
And filent lofe my rapt'rous hour of wit.   160

Quifque tuus quo tenetur conjugali fœdere.
Subter umbras cum maritis ecce balantum gregem.
Et canoras non tacere Diva juffit alites.
Jam loquaces ore rauco ftagna cygni perftrepunt,
Adfonat Terei puellæ fubter umbram populi,
Ut putas motus Amoris ore dici mufico,
Et neges queri fororem de marito barbaro.

   Illa cantat : nos tacemus : quando ver venit meum ?
Quando faciam ut celidon, ut tacere definam ?

'Tis gone; the fit retires; the flames decay;
My tuneful Phœbus flies averſe away.
His own Amycle thus, as ſtories run,
But once was ſilent, and that once undone.
" Let thoſe love now who never lov'd before ; 165
" Let thoſe who always lov'd now love the more."

Perdidi Muſam tacendo, nec me Phœbus reſpicit.
Sic Amyclas, cum tacerent, perdidit ſilentium.
" Cras amet qui numquam amavit ;
" Quique amavit cras amet."

HOMER'S
BATRACHOMUOMACHIA:

OR, THE

BATTLE OF THE FROGS AND MICE.

IN THREE BOOKS.

NAMES OF THE FROGS.	NAMES OF THE MICE.
Physignathus, one who swells his cheeks.	Psycarpax, one who plunders granaries.
Pelus, a name from mud.	Troxartas, a bread-eater.
Hydromeduse, a ruler in the wa- [ters.	Lychomile, a licker of meal.
Hypsiboas, a loud bawler.	Pternotractas, a bacon-eater.
Pelion, from mud.	Lychopinax, a licker of dishes.
Scutlaeus, called from the beets.	Embasichytros, a creeper into pots.
Polyphonus, a great babbler.	
Lymnocharis, one who loves the lake.	Lychenor, a name for licking.
Crambophagus, a cabbage-eater.	Troglodytes, one who runs into holes.
Lymnisius, called from the lake.	Artophagus, who feeds on bread.
Calaminthius, from the herb.	Tyroglyphus, a cheese-scooper.
Hydrocharis, who loves the water.	Pternoglyphus, a bacon-scooper.
Borborocates, who lies in the mud.	Pternophagus, a bacon-eater.
Prassophagus, an eater of garlick.	Cnissodioctes, one who follows the steam of kitchens.
Pelusius, from mud.	
Pelobates, who walks in the dirt.	Sitophagus, an eater of wheat.
Prassaeus, called from garlick.	Meridarpax, one who plunders his share.
Craugasides, from croaking.	

BOOK I.

To fill my rising song with sacred fire,
Ye tuneful Nine, ye sweet celestial quire!
From Helicon's imbow'ring height repair,
Attend my labours, and reward my pray'r:

The dreadful toils of raging Mars I write,   5
The fprings of conteft, and the fields of fight;
How threat'ning Mice advanc'd with warlike grace,
And wag'd dire combats with the croaking race.
Not louder tumults fhook Olympus' tow'rs,
When earth-born giants dar'd immortal pow'rs: 10
Thofe equal acts an equal glory claim,
And thus the Mufe records the tale of fame.

  Once on a time, fatigu'd and out of breath,
And juft efcap'd the ftretching claws of Death,
A gentle Moufe, whom cats purfu'd in vain,   15
Fled fwift-of-foot acrofs the neighb'ring plain,
Hung o'er a brink his eager thirft to cool,
And dipt his whifkers in the ftanding pool;
When near a courteous Frog advanc'd his head,
And from the waters hoarfe-refounding faid: 20
" What art thou, Stranger! what the line you boaft?
" What chance haft caft thee panting on our coaft?
" With ftricteft truth let all thy words agree,
" Nor let me find a faithlefs Moufe in thee.
" If worthy friendfhip, proffer'd friendfhip take, 25
" And ent'ring view the pleafurable lake;
" Range o'er my palace, in my bounty fhare,
" And glad return from hofpitable fare.
" This filver realm extends beneath my fway,
" And me, their monarch, all its Frogs obey.   30
" Great Phyfignathus I! from Peleus' race,
" Begot in fair Hydromede's embrace,

" Where by the nuptial bank that paints his fide,
" The fwift Eridanus delights to glide.   34
" Thee, too, thy form, thy ftrength, and port, pro-
" A fceptred king; a fon of martial fame ;   [claim
" Then trace thy line, and aid my guefling eyes."
Thus ceas'd the Frog, and thus the Moufe replies :
   " Known to the gods, the men, the birds that fly
" Thro' wild expanfes of the midway fky,   40
" My name refounds, and if unknown to thee,
" The foul of great Pfycarpax lives in me.
" Of brave Troxartas' line, whofe fleeky down
" In love comprefs'd Lychomilè the brown.
" My mother fhe, and princefs of the plains   45
" Where'er her father Pternotractas reigns;
" Born where a cabin lifts its airy fhed,
" With figs, with nuts, with vary'd dainties, fed :
" But fince our natures nought in common know,
" From what foundation can a friendfhip grow ? 50
" Thefe curling waters o'er thy palace roll,
" But man's high food fupports my princely foul.
" In vain the circled loaves attempt to lie
" Conceal'd in flafkets from my curious eye ;
" In vain the tripe that boafts the whiteft hue, 55
" In vain the gilded bacon, fhuns my view;
" In vain the cheefes, offspring of the paile,
" Or honey'd cakes, which gods themfelves regale.
" And as in arts I fhine, in arms I fight,
" Mix'd with the braveft, and unknown to flight. 60

" Tho' large to mine the human form appear,
" Not man himself can smite my soul with fear.
" Sly to the bed with silent steps I go,
" Attempt his finger, or attack his toe,
" And fix indented wounds with dex'trous skill; 65
" Sleeping he feels, and only seems to feel.
" Yet have we foes which direful dangers cause,
" Grim owls, with talons arm'd, and cats with claws,
" And that false trap, the den of silent Fate,
" Where Death his ambush plants around the bait: 70
" All-dreaded these, and dreadful o'er the rest
" The potent warriors of the tabby vest ;
" If to the dark we fly, the dark they trace,
" And rend our heroes of the nibbling race;
" But me nor stalks nor watrish herbs delight,   75
" Nor can the crimson radish charm my sight,
" The lake-resounding Frogs' selected fare,
" Which not a Mouse of any taste can bear."
    As thus the downy prince his mind exprest,
His answer thus the croaking king addrest.   80
    " Thy words luxuriant on thy dainties rove,
" And, Stranger, we can boast of bounteous Jove:
" We sport in water, or we dance on land,
" And, born amphibious, food from both command:
" But trust thyself where wonders ask thy view, 85
" And safely tempt those seas, I'll bear thee thro':
" Ascend my shoulders, firmly keep thy seat,
" And reach my marshy court, and feast in state."

He faid, and bent his back; with nimble bound
Leaps the light Moufe, and clafps his arms around, 90
Then wond'ring flotes, and fees with glad furvey
The winding banks refembling ports at fea;
But when aloft the curling water rides,
And wets with azure wave his downy fides,
His thoughts grow confcious of approaching woe, 95
His idle tears with vain repentance flow,
His locks he rends, his trembling feet he rears,
Thick beats his heart with unaccuftom'd fears;
He fighs, and, chill'd with danger, longs for fhore;
His tail extended forms a fruitlefs oar;   100
Half-drench'd in liquid death his pray'rs he fpake,
And thus bemoan'd him from the dreadful lake.

  " So pafs'd Europa thro' the rapid fea,
" Trembling and fainting all the vent'rous way;
" With oary feet the bull triumphant rode,   105
" And fafe in Crete depos'd his lovely load.
" Ah! fafe at laft, may thus the Frog fupport
" My trembling limbs to reach his ample court."

  As thus he forrows, death ambiguous grows;
Lo! from the deep a water-hydra rofe;   110
He rolls his fanguin'd eyes, his bofom heaves,
And darts with active rage along the waves.
Confus'd, the monarch fees his hiffing foe,
And dives, to fhun the fable fates, below.
Forgetful Frog! the friend thy fhoulders bore, 115
Unfkill'd in fwimming, flotes remote from fhore.

He grasps with fruitless hands to find relief,
Supinely falls, and grinds his teeth with grief;
Plunging he sinks, and struggling mounts again,
And sinks, and strives, but strives with Fate in vain;
The weighty moisture clogs his hairy vest,   121
And thus the Prince his dying rage exprest.

 : "Nor thou, that fling'st me flound'ring from thy back,
" As from hard rocks rebounds the shatt'ring wrack,
" Nor thou shalt 'scape thy due, perfidious King! 125
" Pursu'd by vengeance on the swiftest wing.
" At land thy strength could never equal mine;
" At sea to conquer, and by craft, was thine;
" But heav'n has gods, and gods have searching eyes.
" Ye Mice! ye Mice ! my great avengers rise."   130
   This said, he sighing gasp'd, and gasping dy'd.
His death the young Lychopinax espy'd,
As on the flow'ry brink he pass'd the day,
Bask'd in the beams, and loiter'd life away :
Loud shrieks the Mouse, his shrieks the shores repeat;
The nibbling nation learn their hero's fate;   136
Grief, dismal grief, ensues; deep murmurs sound,
And shriller fury fills the deafen'd ground :
From lodge to lodge the sacred heralds run,
To fix their council with the rising sun;   140
Where great Troxartas crown'd in glory reigns,
And winds his length'ning court beneath the plains:
Psycarpax' father, father now no more!
For poor Psycarpax lies remote from shore;

Supine he lies, the silent waters stand,
And no kind billow wafts the dead to land!   146

BOOK II.

WHEN rosy-finger'd Morn had ting'd the clouds,
Around their monarch-Mouse the nation crowds ;
Slow rose the sov'reign, heav'd his anxious breast,
And thus the council, fill'd with rage, addrest.

   " For lost Psycarpax much my soul endures ;   5
" 'Tis mine the private grief, the public yours.
" Three warlike sons adorn'd my nuptial bed,
" Three sons, alas ! before their father dead :
" Our eldest perish'd by the rav'ning cat,
" As near my court the prince unheedful sate ;   10
" Our next an engine fraught with danger drew,
" The portal gap'd, the bait was hung in view;
" Dire arts assist the trap, the Fates decoy,
" And men unpitying kill'd my gallant boy !
" The last, his country's hope, his parents' pride,15
" Plung'd in the lake by Physignathus, dy'd.
" Rouse all the war, my Friends ! avenge the deed,
" And bleed that monarch, and his nation bleed."
   His words in ev'ry breast inspir'd alarms,
And careful Mars supply'd their host with arms. 20
In verdant hulls, despoil'd of all their beans,
The buskin'd warriors stalk'd along the plains :
Quills aptly bound their bracing corselet made,
Fac'd with the plunder of a cat they flay'd ;

The lamp's round bofs affords their ample fhield; 25
Large fhells of nuts their cov'ring helmet yield,
And o'er the region, with reflected rays,
Tall groves of needles for their lances blaze.
Dreadful in arms the marching Mice appear ;
The wond'ring Frogs perceive the tumult near,   30
Forfake the waters, thick'ning form a ring,
And afk and hearken whence the noifes fpring.
When near the crowd, difclos'd to public view,
The valiant chief Embafichytros drew;
The facred herald's fceptre grac'd his hand,   35
And thus his words exprefs'd his king's command.

   " Ye Frogs! the Mice, with vengeance fir'd, advance,
" And, deck'd in armour, fhake the fhining lance ;
" Their haplefs prince by Phyfignathus flain,
" Extends incumbent on the watry plain ;   40
" Then arm your hoft, the doubtful battle try ;
" Lead forth thofe Frogs that have the foul to die."
   The chief retires, the crowd the challenge hear,
And proudly-fwelling, yet perplex'd appear;
Much they refent, yet much their monarch blame, 45
Who rifing, fpoke to clear his tainted fame.

   " O Friends! I never forc'd the Moufe to death,
" Nor faw the gafpings of his lateft breath ;
" He, vain of youth, our art of fwimming try'd,
" And vent'rous, in the lake the wanton dy'd.   50
" To vengeance now by falfe appearance led,
" They point their anger at my guiltlefs head,

" But wage the rifing war by deep device,
" And turn its fury on the crafty Mice.
" Your king directs the way ; my thoughts, elate 55
" With hopes of conqueft, form defigns of fate.
" Where high the banks their verdant furface heave,
" And the fteep fides confine the fleeping wave,
" There, near the margin, clad in armour bright,
" Suftain the firft impetuous fhocks of fight ;   60
" Then where the dancing feather joins the creft,
" Let each brave Frog his obvious Moufe arreft ;
" Each ftrongly grafping, headlong plunge a foe,
" Till countlefs circles whirl the lake below :
" Down fink the Mice in yielding waters drown'd, 65
" Loud flafh the waters, and the fhores refound;
" The Frogs triumphant tread the conquer'd plain,
" And raife their glorious trophies of the flain."
    He fpake no more ; his prudent fcheme imparts
Redoubling ardour to the boldeft hearts.   70
Green was the fuit his arming heroes chofe,
Around their legs the greaves of mallows clofe ;
Green were the beets about their fhoulders laid,
And green the colewort which the target made :
Form'd of the vary'd fhells the waters yield,   75
Their gloffy helmets glift'ned o'er the field;
And tap'ring fea-reeds for the polifh'd fpear,
With upright order pierc'd the ambient air.
Thus drefs'd for war, they take th' appointed height,
Poize the long arms, and urge the promis'd fight. 80
                    I iij

But now, where Jove's irradiate ſpires ariſe,
With ſtars ſurrounded in ethereal ſkies,
(A ſolemn council call'd) the brazen gates
Unbar; the gods aſſume their golden ſeats:
The ſire ſuperior leans, and points to ſhow   85
What wond'rous combats mortals wage below:
How ſtrong, how large, the num'rous heroes ſtride!
What length of lance they ſhake with warlike pride!
What eager fire their rapid march reveals!
So the fierce Centaurs ravag'd o'er the dales;   90
And ſo confirm'd the daring Titans roſe,
Heap'd hills on hills, and bid the gods be foes.

    This ſeen, the pow'r his ſacred viſage rears,
He caſts a pitying ſmile on worldly cares,
And aſks what heav'nly guardians take the liſt,   95
Or who the Mice, or who the Frogs, aſſiſt?
    Then thus to Pallas. " If my daughter's mind
" Have join'd the Mice, why ſtays ſhe ſtill behind?
" Drawn forth by ſav'ry ſteams they wind their way,
" And ſure attendance round thine altar pay,   100
" Where while the victims gratify their taſte,
" They ſport to pleaſe the goddeſs of the feaſt."
    Thus ſpake the ruler of the ſpacious ſkies;
But thus, reſolv'd, the blue-ey'd maid replies.
" In vain, my Father! all their dangers plead,   105
" To ſuch thy Pallas never grants her aid:
" My flow'ry wreaths they petulantly ſpoil,
" And rob my cryſtal lamps of feeding oil;

" (Ills following ills!) but what afflicts me more,
" My veil that idle race profanely tore :   110
" The web was curious, wrought with art divine;
" Relentlefs Wretches! all the work was mine!
" Along the loom the purple warp I fpread,
" Caft the light fhoot, and crofs'd the filver thread;
" In this their teeth a thoufand breaches tear,   115
" The thoufand breaches fkilful hands repair,
" For which vile earthly duns thy daughter grieve,
" (The gods, that ufe no coin, have none to give,
" And learning's goddefs never lefs can owe,
" Neglected learning gains no wealth below.)   120
" Nor let the Frogs to win my fuccour fue ;
" Thofe clam'rous fools have loft my favour too :
" For late, when all the conflicts ceaft at night,
" When my ftretch'd finews work'd with eager fight;
" When, fpent with glorious toil, I left the field, 125
" And funk for flumber on my fwelling fhield,
" Lo, from the deep, repelling fweet repofe,
" With noify croakings half the nation rofe :
" Devoid of reft, with akeing brows I lay,
" Till cocks proclaim'd the crimfon dawn of day. 130
" Let all, like me, from either hoft forbear,
" Nor tempt the flying furies of the fpear,
" Left heav'nly blood (or what for blood may flow)
" Adorn the conqueft of a meaner foe.   134
" Some daring Moufe may meet the wondrous odds,
" Tho' gods oppofe, and brave the wounded gods:

" O'er gilded clouds reclin'd the danger view,
" And be the wars of mortal fcenes for you."
    So mov'd the blue-ey'd Queen; her words perfuade,
Great Jove affented, and the reft obey'd.   140

BOOK III.

Now front to front the marching armies fhine,
Halt ere they meet, and form the length'ning line:
The chiefs confpicuous feen, and heard afar,
Give the loud fignal to the rufhing war;
Their dreadful trumpets deep-mouth'd hornets found,
The founded charge remurmurs o'er the ground;   6
Ev'n Jove proclaims a field of horror nigh,
And rolls low thunder thro' the troubled fky.
    Firft to the fight the large Hypfiboas fiew,
And brave Lychenor with a javelin flew: 10
The lucklefs warrior, fill'd with gen'rous flame,
Stood foremoft glitt'ring in the poft of fame,
When in his liver ftruck the jav'lin hung,
The Moufe fell thund'ring, and the target rung;
Prone to the ground he finks his clofing eye,   15
And foil'd in duft his lovely treffes lie.
    A fpear at Pelion Troglodytes caft,
The miffive fpear within the bofom paft;
Death's fable fhades the fainting Frog furround,
And life's red tide runs ebbing from the wound.   20
Embafichytros felt Scutlæus' dart
Transfix and quiver in his panting heart;

But great Artophagus aveng'd the flain,
And big Scutlæus tumbling loads the plain:
And Polyphonus dies, a Frog renown'd   25
For boaftful fpeech and turbulence of found;
Deep thro' the belly pierc'd, fupine he lay,
And breath'd his foul againft the face of day.

    The ftrong Lymnocharis, who view'd with ire
A victor triumph and a friend expire,   30
With heaving arms a rocky fragment caught,
And fiercely flung where Troglodytes fought,
(A warrior vers'd in arts of fure retreat,
But arts in vain elude impending fate)
Full on his finewy neck the fragment fell,   35
And o'er his eyelids clouds eternal dwell.
Lychenor (fecond of the glorious name)
Striding advanc'd, and took no wand'ring aim;
Thro' all the Frog the fhining jav'lin flies,
And near the vanquifh'd Moufe the victor dies.   40

    The dreadful ftroke Crambophagus affrights,
Long bred to banquets, lefs inur'd to fights;
Heedlef he runs, and ftumbles o'er the fteep,
And wildly flound'ring flafhes up the deep;
Lychenor following with a downward blow,   45
Reach'd in the lake his unrecover'd foe;
Gafping he rolls, a purple ftream of blood
Diftains the furface of the filver flood;
Thro' the wide wound the rufhing entrails throng,
And flow the breathlefs carcafs flotes along.   50

Lymnifius good Tyroglyphus affails,
Prince of the Mice that haunt the flow'ry vales ;
Loft to the milky fares and rural feat,
He came to perifh on the bank of Fate.

    The dread Pternoglyphus demands the fight,   55
Which tender Calaminthius fhuns by flight ;
Drops the green target, fpringing quits the foe,
Glides thro' the lake, and fafely dives below;
But dire Pternophagus divides his way
Thro' breaking ranks, and leads the dreadful day. 60
No nibbling prince excell'd in fiercenefs more,
His parents fed him on the favage boar;
But where his lance the field with blood imbru'd,
Swift as he mov'd Hydrocharis purfu'd,
Till fall'n in death he lies; a fhatt'ring ftone   65
Sounds on the neck, and crufhes all the bone ;
His blood pollutes the verdure of the plain,
And from his noftrils burfts the gufhing brain.

    Lychopinax with Borborocates fights,
A blamelefs Frog, whom humbler life delights;   70
The fatal jav'lin unrelenting flies,
And darknefs feals the gentle croaker's eyes.

    Incens'd Praffophagus with fpritely bound
Bears Cniffodioctes off the rifing ground,
Then drags him o'er the lake depriv'd of breath, 75
And downward plunging, finks his foul to death.
But now the great Pfycarpax fhines afar,
(Scarce he fo great whofe lofs provok'd the war)

Swift to revenge his fatal jav'lin fled,
And thro' the liver struck Pelusius dead;   80
His freckled corpse before the victor fell,
His soul indignant sought the shades of hell.

This saw Pelobates, and from the flood
Heav'd with both hands a monstrous mass of mud;
The cloud obscene o'er all the hero flies,   85
Dishonours his brown face, and blots his eyes:
Enrag'd, and wildly sputt'ring, from the shore
A stone immense of size the warrior bore,
A load for lab'ring earth, (whose bulk to raise
Asks ten degen'rate Mice of modern days)   90
Full on the leg arrives the crushing wound;
The Frog-supportless writhes upon the ground.

Thus flush'd, the victor wars with matchless force,
Till loud Craugasides arrests his course:
Hoarse-croaking threats precede; with fatal speed 95
Deep thro' the belly run the pointed reed,
Then strongly tugg'd, return'd imbru'd with gore,
And on the pile his reeking entrails bore.

The lame Sitophagus, oppress'd with pain,
Creeps from the desp'rate dangers of the plain;   100
And where the ditches rising weeds supply
To spread their lowly shades beneath the sky,
There lurks the silent Mouse reliev'd from heat,
And, safe embower'd, avoids the chance of Fate.

But here Troxartas, Physignathus there,   105
Whirl the dire furies of the pointed spear;

But where the foot around its ankle plies,
Troxartas wounds, and Physignathus flies,
Halts to the pool, a safe retreat to find,
And trails a dangling length of leg behind;   110
The Moufe still urges, still the Frog retires,
And half in anguish of the flight expires.

    Then pious ardour young Praffæus brings
Betwixt the fortunes of contending kings;
Lank, harmlefs Frog! with forces hardly grown, 115
He darts the reed in combats not his own,
Which faintly tinkling on Troxartas' shield,
Hangs at the point, and drops upon the field.

    Now nobly tow'ring o'er the reft appears
A gallant prince, that far tranfcends his years, 120
Pride of his fire, and glory of his house,
And more a Mars in combat than a Moufe;
His action bold, robuft his ample fiame,
And Meridarpax his refounding name.
The warrior, fingled from the fighting crowd, 125
Boafts the dire honours of his arms aloud:
Then ftrutting near the lake, with looks elate,
To all its nations threats approaching fate:
And fuch his ftrength, the filver lakes around
Might roll their waters o'er unpeopled ground: 130
But pow'rful Jove, who shews no lefs his grace
To Frogs that perish than to human race,
Felt foft compaffion rifing in his foul,
And shook his facred head, that shook the pole;

  5

Then thus to all the gazing pow'rs began   135
The fire of gods, and Frogs, and Mice, and man.
    " What feas of blood I view! what worlds of flain!
" An Iliad rifing from a day's campaign!
" How fierce his jav'lin o'er the trembling lakes
" The black-furr'd hero Meridarpax fhakes!   140
" Unlefs fome fav'ring deity defcend,
" Soon will the Frogs' loquacious empire end.
" Let dreadful Pallas, wing'd with pity, fly,
" And make her ægis blaze before his eye,
" While Mars refulgent on his rattling car   145
" Arrefts his raging rival of the war."
    He ceas'd, reclining with attentive head,
When thus the glorious god of combats faid:
" Nor Pallas, Jove, tho' Pallas take the field
" With all the terrors of her hiffing fhield,   150
" Nor Mars himfelf, tho' Mars in armour bright
" Afcend his car, and wheel amidft the fight;
" Not thefe can drive the defp'rate Moufe afar,
" Or change the fortunes of the bleeding war;
" Let all go forth, all heav'n in arms arife,   155
" Or launch thy own red thunder from the fkies;
" Such ardent bolts as flew that wondrous day,
" When heaps of Titans mix'd with mountains lay,
" When all the giant-race enormous fell,
" And huge Enceladus was hurl'd to hell."   160
    'Twas thus th' armipotent advis'd the gods,
When from his throne the Cloud-compeller nods;

Deep length'ning thunders run from pole to pole,
Olympus trembles as the thunders roll:
Then fwift he whirls the brandifh'd bolt around, 165
And headlong darts it at the diftant ground;
The bolt difcharg'd, inwrapp'd with lightning, flies,
And rends its flaming paffage thro' the fkies,
Then earth's inhabitants, the Nibblers, fhake,
And Frogs, the dwellers in the waters, quake: 170
Yet ftill the Mice advance their dread defign,
And the laft danger threats the croaking line,
Till Jove, that inly mourn'd the lofs they bore,
With ftrange affiftants fill'd the frighted fhore. 174

   Pour'd from the neighb'ring ftrand, deform'd to
They march, a fudden unexpected crew!   [view,
Strong fuits of armour round their bodies clofe,
Which like thick anvils blunt the force of blows;
In wheeling marches turn'd oblique they go;
With harpy claws their limbs divide below;   180
Fell fheers the paffage to their mouth command;
From out the flefh their bones by nature ftand;
Broad fpread their backs, their fhining fhoulders rife;
Unnumber'd joints diftort their lengthen'd thighs;
With nervous cords their hands are firmly brac'd:185
Their round black eyeballs in their bofom plac'd;
On eight long feet the wondrous warriors tread,
And either end alike fupplies a head:
Thefe mortal wits to call the Crabs agree;
The gods have other names for things than we. 190

Now where the jointures from their loins depend,
The heroes' tails with fev'ring grafps they rend;
Here fhort of feet, depriv'd the pow'r to fly,
There without hands, upon the field they lie :
Wrench'd from their holds, and fcatter'd all around,
The bended lances heap the cumber'd ground.   196
Helplefs amazement, fear purfuing fear,
And mad confufion thro' their hoft appear;
O'er the wild wafte with headlong flight they go,
Or creep conceal'd in vaulted holes below.   200
But down Olympus to the weftern feas
Far-fhooting Phœbus drove with fainter rays,
And a whole war (fo Jove ordain'd) begun,
Was fought, and ceas'd, in one revolving fun.   204

THE RAPE OF THE LOCK.

And now unveil'd, the toilette stands display'd,
Each silver vase in mystic order laid.
First, rob'd in white, the Nymph intent adores,
With head uncover'd, the cosmetic pow'rs.
A heav'nly image in the glass appears,   *5*
To that she bends, to that her eyes she rears:
Th' inferior priestess, at her altar's side,
Trembling begins the sacred rites of pride.

A translation of part of the first Canto of

THE RAPE OF THE LOCK

Into Leonine verse, after the manner of the ancient Monks.

Er nunc dilectum speculum, pro more retectum,
Emicat in mensâ, quæ splendet pyxide densâ:
Tum primum lymphâ, se purgat candida Nympha;
Jamque sine mendâ, cœlestis imago videnda,
Nuda caput, bellos retinet, regit, implet, ocellos.
Hâc stupet explorans, seu cultus numen adorans.
Inferior claram Pythonissa apparet ad aram,

Unnumber'd treasures ope at once, and here
The various off'rings of the world appear;   10
From each she nicely culls with curious toil,
And decks the goddess with the glitt'ring spoil.
This casket India's glowing gems unlocks,
And all Arabia breathes from yonder box.
The tortoise here and elephant unite,   15
Transform'd to combs, the speckled and the white.
Here files of pins extend their shining rows,
Puffs, powders, patches, Bibles, billet-doux.
Now awful Beauty puts on all its arms,
The fair each moment rises in her charms,   20

Fertque tibi cautè, dicatque superbia! lautè,
Dona venusta; oris, quæ cunctis, plena laboris,
Excerpta explorat, dominamque deamque decorat.
Pyxide devotâ, se pandit hic India tota,
Et tota ex istâ transpirat Arabia cistâ;
Testudo hic flectit, dum se mea Lesbia pectit;
Atque elephas lentè, te pectit Lesbia dente;
Hunc maculis nôris, nivei jacet ille coloris.
Hic jacet et mundè, mundus muliebris abundè;
Spinula resplendens æris longo ordine pendens,
Pulvis suavis odore, et epistola suavis amore.
Induit arma ergo, Veneris pulcherrima virgo;
Pulchrior in præsens tempus de tempore crescens;

Repairs her fmiles, awakens ev'ry grace,
And calls forth all the wonders of her face;
Sees by degrees a purer blufh arife,
And keener lightnings quicken in her eyes.
The bufy Sylphs furround their darling care,   25
Thefe fet the head, and thofe divide the hair;
Some fold the fleeve, while others plait the gown,
And Betty's prais'd for laboors not her own.   28

Jam reparat rifus, jam furgit gratiâ vifûs,
Jam promit cultu, mirac'la latentia vultu.
Pigmina jam mifcet, quo plus fua purpura glifcet,
Et geminans bellis fplendet magè fulgor ocellis.
Stant lemures muti, Nymphæ intentique faluti,
Hic figit Zonam, capiti locat ille coronam,
Hæc manicis formam, plicis datet altera normam:
Et tibi vel Betty, tibi vel nitidiffima Letty!
Gloria factorum temerê conceditur horum.

AN ELEGY.

TO AN OLD BEAUTY.

In vain, poor Nymph! to pleafe our youthful fight,
You fleep in cream and frontlets all the night,
Your face with patches foil, with paint repair,
Drefs with gay gowns, and fhade with foreign hair :
If truth in fpight of manners muft be told,　　　5
Why, really fifty-five is fomething old.

　Once you were young, or one, whofe life's fo long
She might have born my mother, tells me wrong :
And once (fince Envy's dead before you die)
The women own you play'd a fparkling eye,　　　10
Taught the light foot a modifh little trip,
And pouted with the prettieft purple lip.———

　To fome new charmer are the rofes fled,
Which blew to damafk all thy cheek with red ;
Youth calls the Graces there to fix their reign,　　15
And airs by thoufands fill their eafy train.
So parting Summer bids her flow'ry prime
Attend the fun to drefs fome foreign clime,
While with'ring feafons in fucceffion, here,
Strip the gay gardens, and deform the year.　　　20

　But thou (fince Nature bids) the world refign,
'Tis now thy daughter's daughter's time to fhine ;
With more addrefs, (or fuch as pleafes more)
She runs her female exercifes o'er,

Unfurls or clofes, raps or turns the fan,   25
And fmiles, or blufhes, at the creature Man:
With quicker life, as gilded coaches pafs,
In fideling courtefy fhe drops the glafs:
With better ftrength, on vifit-days, fhe bears
To mount her fifty flights of ample ftairs.   30
Her mien, her fhape, her temper, eyes, and tongue,
Are fure to conquer,—for the rogue is young;
And all that's madly wild or oddly gay,
We call it only pretty Fanny's way.   34

    Let time, that makes you homely, make you fage;
The fphere of wifdom is the fphere of age.
'Tis true, when beauty dawns with early fire,
And hears the flatt'ring tongues of foft defire,
If not from virtue, from its graveft ways
The foul with pleafing avocation ftrays;   40
But beauty gone 'tis eafier to be wife,
As harpers better by the lofs of eyes.

    Henceforth retire, reduce your roving airs,
Haunt lefs the plays, and more the public pray'rs;
Rejeft the Mechlin head and gold brocade,   45
Go pray, in fober Norwich crape array'd.
Thy pendent di'monds let thy Fanny take,
(Their trembling luftre fhows how much you fhake)
Or bid her wear thy necklace row'd with pearl,
You'll find your Fanny an obedient girl.   50
So for the reft, with lefs incumbrance hung,
You walk thro' life unmingled with the young,

And view the fhade and fubftance as you pafs,
With joint endeavour trifling at the glafs,
Or Folly drefs'd, and rambling all her days,   55
To meet her counterpart, and grow by praife;
Yet ftill fedate your felf, and gravely plain,
You neither fret nor envy at the vain.

  'Twas thus (if man with woman we compare)
The wife Athenian crofs'd a glittering fair;   60
Unmov'd by tongues and fights he walk'd the place,
Thro' tape, toys, tinfel, gimp, perfume, and lace,
Then bends from Mars's Hill his awful eyes,
And " what a world I never want?" he cries;
But cries unheard; for Folly will be free;   65
So parts the buzzing gaudy crowd and he:
As carelefs he for them as they for him;
He wrapt in wifdom, and they whirl'd by whim. 68

THE BOOK-WORM.

Come hither, Boy! we'll hunt to-day
The Book-worm, ravening beaſt of prey,
Produc'd by parent Earth, at odds
(As Fame reports it) with the gods.
Him frantic hunger wildly drives   5
Againſt a thouſand authors' lives:
Thro' all the fields of wit he flies;
Dreadful his head with cluſt'ring eyes,
With horns without, and tuſks within,
And ſcales to ſerve him for a ſkin.   10
Obſerve him nearly, leſt he climb
To wound the bards of ancient time,
Or down the vale of Fancy go
To tear ſome modern wretch below;
On ev'ry corner fix thine eye,   15
Or ten to one he ſlips thee by.
    See where his teeth a paſſage eat;
We'll rouſe him from the deep retreat.
But who the ſhelter's forc'd to give?
'Tis ſacred Virgil, as I live!   20
From leaf to leaf, from ſong to ſong,
He draws the tadpole form along,
He mounts the gilded edge before,
He's up, he ſcuds the cover o'er;
He turns, he doubles; there he paſt,   25
And here we have him caught at laſt.

Infatiate Brute! whofe teeth abufe
The fweeteft fervants of the Mufe.
(Nay, never offer to deny,
I took thee in the fact to fly.)   30
His rofes nipt in ev'ry page,
My poor Anacreon mourns thy rage;
By thee my Ovid wounded lies;
By thee my Lefbia's Sparrow dies;
Thy rabid teeth have half deftroy'd   35
The work of Love in Biddy Floyd;
They rent Belinda's locks away,
And fpoil'd the Blouzelind of Gay.
For all, for ev'ry fingle deed,
Relentlefs Juftice bids thee bleed.   40
Then fall a victim to the Nine,
Myfelf the prieft, my defk the fhrine.
    Bring Homer, Virgil, Taffo, near,
To pile a facred altar here.
Hold, Boy! thy hand out-runs thy wit,   45
You reach'd the plays that D————s writ;
You reach'd me Ph————s ruftic ftrain;
Pray take your mortal bards again.
    Come, bind the victim————There he lies,
And here between his num'rous eyes   50
This venerable duft I lay,
From manufcripts juft fwept away.
    The goblet in my hand I take,
(For the libation's yet to make)

A health to Poets! all their days   55
May they have bread as well as praife;
Senfe may they feek, and lefs engage
In papers fill'd with party-rage;
But if their riches fpoil their vein,
Ye Mufes! make them poor again.   60

 Now bring the weapon, yonder blade,
With which my tuneful pens are made.
I ftrike the fcales that arm thee round,
And twice and thrice I print the wound;
The facred altar flotes with red,   65
And now he dies, and now he's dead.

 How like the fon of Jove I ftand,
This hydra ftretch'd beneath my hand!
Lay bare the monfter's entrails here,
To fee what dangers threat the year: 70
Ye Gods! what Sonnets on a wench!
What lean Tranflations out of French!
'Tis plain, this lobe is fo unfound,·
S——— prints before the months go round.

 But hold, before I clofe the fcene,   75
The facred altar fhould be clean.
Oh! had I Sh———ll's fecond bays,
Or, T———! thy pert and humble lays,
(Ye Pair! forgive me when I vow
I never mifs'd your Works till now)   80
I'd tear the leaves to wipe the fhrine,
(That only way you pleafe the Nine)

4

But since I chance to want these two,
I'll make the songs of D——y do.

    Rent from the corpse, on yonder pin   85
I hang the scales that brac'd it in ;
I hang my studious morning gown,
And write my own inscription down.

    " This trophy, from the Python won,
" This robe, in which the deed was done,   90
" These Parnell, glorying in the feat,
" Hung on these shelves, the Muses' feat.
" Here Ignorance and Hunger found
" Large realms of wit to ravage round ;
" Here Ignorance and Hunger fell ;   ·95
" Two foes in one I sent to hell.
" Ye Poets ! who my labours see,
" Come share the triumph all with me:
" Ye Critics ! born to vex the Muse,
" Go mourn the grand ally you lose."   100

AN ALLEGORY ON MAN.

A THOUGHTFUL being, long and fpare,
Our race of mortals call him Care,
(Were Homer living, well he knew
What name the gods have call'd him too)
With fine mechanic genius wrought,   5
And lov'd to work, tho' no one bought.
  This being, by a model bred
In Jove's eternal fable head,
Contriv'd a fhape impower'd to breathe,
And be the worldling here beneath.   10
  The man rofe ftaring, like a ftake,
Wond'ring to fee himfelf awake!
Then look'd fo wife, before he knew
The bus'nefs he was made to do,
That pleas'd to fee with what a grace   15
He gravely fhew'd his forward face,
Jove talk'd of breeding him on high,
An under-fomething of the fky.
  But ere he gave the mighty nod,
Which ever binds a poet's god,   20
(For which his curls ambrofial fhake,
And Mother Earth's oblig'd to quake)
He faw old Mother Earth arife,
She ftood confefs'd before his eyes,
But not with what we read fhe wore,   25
A caftle for a crown before,

Nor with long ſtreets and longer roads,
Dangling behind her like commodes:
As yet with wreaths alone ſhe dreſt,
And trail'd a landſcape-painted veſt;   30
Then thrice ſhe rais'd. (as Ovid ſaid)
And thrice ſhe bow'd, her weighty head.
    Her honours made, " Great Jove," ſhe cry'd,
" This thing was faſhion'd from my ſide;
" His hands, his heart, his head, are mine,   35
" Then what haſt thou to call him thine,"
   " Nay rather ask," the monarch ſaid,
" What boots his hand, his heart, his head?
" Were what I gave remov'd away,
" Thy part's an idle ſhape of clay."   40
   " Halves, more than halves," cry'd honeſt Care,
" Your pleas would make your titles fair;
" You claim the body, you the ſoul,
" But I who join'd them claim the whole."
   Thus with the gods debate began   45
On ſuch a trivial cauſe as Man.
" And can celeſtial tempers rage?"
Quoth Virgil, in a latter age.
   As thus they wrangled, Time came by;
(There's none that paint him ſuch as I,   50
For what the fabling Ancients ſung
Makes Saturn old when Time was young.)
As yet his winters had not ſhed
Their ſilver honours on his head;
               L ij

He juſt had got his pinions free   55
From his old ſire Eternity.
A ſerpent girdled round he wore,
The tail within the mouth before,
By which our almanacs are clear
That learned Egypt meant the year.   60
A ſtaff he carry'd, where on high
A glaſs was fix'd to meaſure by,
As amber boxes made a ſhow
For heads of canes an age ago.
His veſt, for day and night, was py'd,   65
A bending ſickle arm'd his ſide,
And Spring's new months his train adorn ;
The other ſeaſons were unborn.
   Known by the gods, as near he draws,
They make him umpire of the cauſe.   70
O'er a low trunk his arm he laid,
(Where ſince his hours a dial made)
Then leaning heard the nice debate,
And thus pronounc'd the words of Fate.
   " Since body from the parent Earth,   75
" And ſoul from Jove, receiv'd a birth,
" Return they where they firſt began;
" But ſince their union makes the man,
" Till Jove and Earth ſhall part theſe two,
" To Care, who join'd them, Man is due."   80
      He ſaid, and ſprung with ſwift career
To trace a circle for the year;

Where ever fince the feafons wheel,
And tread on one another's heel.
    " 'Tis well," faid Jove; and for confent   85
Thund'ring he fhook the firmament.
" Our umpire Time fhall have his way,
" With Care I let the creature ftay :
" Let bus'nefs vex him, av'rice blind,
" Let doubt and knowledge rack his mind;   90
" Let Error act, Opinion fpeak,
" And Want afflict, and Sicknefs break,
" And anger burn, Dejection chill,
" And Joy diftract, and Sorrow kill ;
" Till arm'd by Care, and taught to mow,   95
" Time draws the long deftructive blow,
" And wafted man, whofe quick decay
" Comes hurrying on before his day,
" Shall only find, by this decree,
" The foul flies fooner back to me."   100

.

SOME FRENCH VERSES.

Relentless Time! deftroying pow'r
Whom ftone and brafs obey,
Who giv'ft to ev'ry flying hour
To work fome new decay;

Unheard, unheeded, and unfeen,   5
Thy fecret faps prevail,
And ruin man, a nice machine,
By Nature form'd to fail.

My change arrives: the change I meet
Before I thought it nigh: 10
My fpring, my years of pleafure fleet,
And all their beauties die.

In age I fearch, and only find
A poor unfruitful gain,
Grave Wifdom ftalking flow behind,   15
Opprefs'd with loads of pain.

My ignorance could once beguile,
And fancy'd joys infpire;
My errors cherifh'd Hope to fmile
On newly-born Defire: 20

But now experience shews the blifs
For which I fondly fought
Not worth the long impatient wish
And ardour of the thought.

My youth met Fortune fair array'd,   25
(In all her pomp she shone)
And might, perhaps, have well effay'd
To make her gifts my own:

But when I faw the bleffings show'r
On fome unworthy mind,   30
I left the chace, and own'd the pow'r
Was juftly painted blind.

I pafs'd the glories which adorn
The fplendid courts of kings,
And while the perfons mov'd my fcorn,   35
I rofe to fcorn the things.

My manhood felt a vig'rous fire,
By love increas'd the more;
But years with coming years confpire
To break the chains I wore.   40

In weaknefs fafe, the fex I fee
With idle luftre fhine;
For what are all their joys to me,
Which cannot now be mine?

But hold——I feel my gout decreafe,   45
My troubles laid to reft ;
And truths which would difturb my peace
Are painful truths at beft.

Vainly the time I have to roll
In fad reflection flies ;   50
Ye fondling Paffions of my foul!
Ye fweet Deceits! arife.

I wifely change the fcene within
To things that us'd to pleafe ;
In pain philofophy is fpleen,
In health 'tis only eafe.   56

A NIGHT-PIECE ON DEATH.

By the blue taper's trembling light
No more I wafte the wakeful night,
Intent with endlefs view to pore
The fchoolmen and the fages o'er ;
Their books from wifdom widely ftray,   5
Or point at beft the longeft way :
I'll feek a readier path, and go
Where wifdom's furely taught below.
   How deep yon' azure dies the fky !
Where orbs of gold unnumber'd lie,   10

While thro' their ranks, in filver pride,
The nether crefcent feems to glide.
The flumb'ring breeze forgets to breathe,
The lake is fmooth and clear beneath;
Where once again the fpangled fhow   15
Defcends to meet our eyes below,
The grounds which on the right afpire,
In dimnefs from the view retire;
The left prefents a place of graves,✔
Whofe wall the filent water laves.   20
That fteeple guides thy doubtful fight
Among the livid gleams of night;
There pafs, with melancholy ftate,
By all the folemn heaps of Fate,
And think, as foftly-fad you tread   25
Above the venerable dead,
" Time was like thee they life poffefr,
" And time fhall be that thou fhalt reft '
-Thofe graves, with bending ofier bound,
That namelefs heave the crumbled ground,   30
Quick to the glancing thought difclofe
Where Toil and Poverty repofe.
    The flat fmooth ftones that bear a name,
The chiffel's flender help to fame,
(Which ere our fett of friends decay   35
Their frequent fteps may wear away)
A middle race of mortals own,
Men half ambitious, all unknown.

The marble tombs that rife on high,
Whofe dead in vaulted arches lie,   40
Whofe pillars fwell with fculptur'd ftones,
Arms, angels, epitaphs, and bones,
Thefe (all the poor remains of ftate)
Adorn the rich or praife the great,
Who while on earth in fame they live,   45
Are fenfelefs of the fame they give.

 Ha! while I gaze pale Cynthia fades,
The burfting earth unveils the fhades!
All flow, and wan, and wrapp'd with fhrouds,
They rife in vifionary crowds,   50
And all with fober accent cry,
" Think, Mortal! what it is to die."

 Now from yon' black and fun'ral yew,
That bathes the charnel-houfe with dew,
Methinks I hear a voice begin;   55
(Ye Ravens! ceafe your croaking din;
Ye tolling Clocks! no time refound
O'er the long lake and midnight ground)
It fends a peal of hollow groans,
Thus fpeaking from among the bones.   60

 " When men my fcythe and darts fupply,
" How great a king of fears am I!
" They view me like the laft of things;
" They make, and then they dread, my ftings.
" Fools! if you lefs provok'd your fears,   65
" No more my fpectre-form appears.

" Death's but a path that muſt be trod,
" If man would ever paſs to God;
" A port of calms, a ſtate of eaſe
" From the rough rage of ſwelling ſeas."   70
  Why then thy flowing ſable ſtoles,
Deep pendent cypreſs, mourning poles,
Looſe ſcarfs to fall athwart thy weeds,
Long palls, drawn herſes, cover'd ſteeds,
And plumes of black, that, as they tread,   75
Nod o'er the 'ſcutcheons of the dead?
  Nor can the parted body know,
Nor wants the ſoul, theſe forms of woe.
As men who long in priſon dwell,
With lamps that glimmer round the cell,   80
Whene'er their ſuff'ring years are run,
Spring forth to greet the glitt'ring ſun;
Such joy, tho' far tranſcending ſenſe,
Have pious ſouls at parting hence.
On earth, and in the body plac'd,   85
A few and evil years they waſte;
But when their chains are caſt aſide,
See the glad ſcene unfolding wide,
Clap the glad wing, and tow'r away,
And mingle with the blaze of day.   90

THE HORSE AND THE OLIVE.

With moral tale let ancient wifdom move,
Whilft thus I fing to make the Moderns wife;
Strong Neptune once with fage Minerva ftrove,
And rifing Athens was the victor's prize.

By Neptune Plutus, (guardian pow'r of gain)   5
By great Minerva bright Apollo ftood;
But Jove fuperior bade the fide obtain
Which beft contriv'd to do the nation good.

Then Neptune ftriking, from the parted ground
The warlike Horfe came pawing on the plain,   10
And as it tofs'd its mane and pranc'd around,
" By this," he cries, " I'll make the people reign."

The goddefs, fmiling, gently bow'd her fpear,
" And rather thus they fhall be blefs'd," fhe faid:
Then upwards fhooting in the vernal air,   15
With loaded boughs the fruitful Olive fpread.

Jove faw what gift the rural pow'rs defign'd,
And took th' impartial fcales, refolv'd to fhow
If greater blifs in warlike pomp we find,
Or in the calm which peaceful times beftow.   20

On Neptune's part he plac'd victorious days,
Gay trophies won, and fame extending wide;
But Plenty, Safety, Science, Arts, and Eafe,
Minerva's fcale with greater weight fupply'd.

Fierce War devours whom gentle Peace would fave;
Sweet Peace reftores what angry War deftroys;   26
War made for peace with that rewards the brave,
While peace its pleafures from itfelf enjoys.

Hence vanquifh'd Neptune to the fea withdrew,
Hence wife Minerva rul'd Athenian lands;   30
Her Athens hence in arts and honours grew,
And ftill her Olives deck pacific hands.

From fables thus difclos'd, a monarch's mind
May form juft rules to chufe the truly great,
And fubjects, weary'd with diftreffes, find   35
Whofe kind endeavours moft befriend the ftate.

Ev'n Britain here may learn to place her love,
If cities won her kingdom's wealth have coft;
If Anna's thoughts the patriot fouls approve,
Whofe cares reftore that wealth the wars had loft. 40

But if we afk, the moral to difclofe,
Whom her beft patronefs Europa calls,
Volume I.   M

Great Anna's title no exception knows,
And unapply'd in this the fable falls.

With her nor Neptune or Minerva vies: 45
Whene'er fhe pleas'd her troops to conqueft flew ;
Whene'er fhe pleafes peaceful times arife :
She gave the Horfe, and gives the Olive too.   48

THE THIRD SATIRE

OF DR. DONNE.

VERSIFIED BY DR. PARNELL.

Compassion checks my spleen, yet scorn denies
The tears a passage through my swelling eyes;
To laugh or weep at sins might idly show
Unheedful passion or unfruitful woe.
Satire ! arise, and try thy sharper ways,   5
If ever satire cur'd an old disease.
Is not Religion (heav'n-descended dame!)
As worthy all our soul's devoutest flame,
As Moral Virtue in her early sway,
When the best Heathens saw by doubtful day ?   10

THE THIRD SATIRE

OF DR. DONNE.

Kind Pity checks my spleen, brave Scorn forbids
Those tears to issue which swell my eye-lids.
I must not laugh nor weep sins, but be wise,
Can railing then cure these worn maladies ?
Is not our mistress, fair Religion,
As worthy of all our soul's devotion
As Virtue was to the first blinded age ?
Are not heaven's joyes as valiant to assuage

Are not the joys, the promis'd joys above,
As great and ftrong to vanifh earthly love
As earthly glory, fame, refpect, and fhow,
As all rewards their virtue found below?
Alas! Religion proper means prepares,   15
Thefe means are ours, and muft its end be theirs?
And fhall thy father's fpirit meet the fight
Of Heathen fages cloth'd in heav'nly light,
Whofe merit of ftrict life, feverely fuited
To Reafon's dictates, may be faith imputed,   20
Whilft thou, to whom he taught the nearer road,
Art ever banifh'd from the blefs'd abode?

   Oh! if thy temper fuch a fear can find,
This fear were valour of the nobleft kind.

   Dar'ft thou provoke, when rebel-fouls afpire,   25
Thy Maker's vengeance and thy monarch's ire,
Or live entomb'd in fhips, thy leader's prey,
Spoil of the war, the famine, or the fea;

Lufts, as earth's honour was to them? Alas!
As we do them in means, fhall they furpafs
Us in the end? and fhall thy father's fpirit
Meet blind philofophers in heaven, whofe merit
Of ftrict life may be imputed faith, and hear
Thee, whom he taught fo eafie wayes and near
To follow, damn'd? Oh! if thou dar'ft, fear this:
This fear great courage and high valour is.
Dar'ft thou ayd mutinous Dutch? and dar'ft thou lay
Thee in fhips, wooden fepulchres, a prey

In fearch of pearl in depth of ocean breathe,
Or live, exil'd the fun, in mines beneath,   30
Or where in tempefts icy mountains roll,
Attempt a paffage by the northern pole?
Or dar'ft thou parch within the fires of Spain,
Or burn beneath the line for Indian gain?
Or for fome idol of thy fancy draw   35
Some loofe-gown'd dame? O courage made of ftraw!
Thus, defp'rate Coward! would'ft thou bold appear,
Yet when thy God has plac'd thee centry here,
To thy own foes, to his, ignoble yield,
And leave, for wars forbid, th' appointed field?   40

To leaders' rage, to ftorms, to fhot, to dearth?
Dar'ft thou dive feas and dungeons of the earth?
Haft thou courageous fire to thaw the ice
Of frozen North difcoveries, and thrice
Colder than falamanders? like divine
Children in th' oven, fires of Spain and the line,
Whofe countries limbecks to our bodies be,
Canft thou for gain bear? and muft every he
Which cries not Goddefs to thy miftrefs draw
Or eat thy poyfonous words : Courage of ftraw!
O defperate Coward! wilt thou feem bold, and
To thy foes and his (who made thee to ftand
Sentinel in this world's garrifon) thus yield,
And for forbid warres leave th' appointed field?

M iij

Know thy own foes; th'apoſtate Angel, he
You ſtrive to pleaſe, the foremoſt of the three;
He makes the pleaſures of his realm the bait,
But can he give for love that acts in hate?
The World's thy ſecond love, thy ſecond foe,   45
The World, whoſe beauties periſh as they blow;
They fly, ſhe fades herſelf, and at the beſt,
You graſp a wither'd ſtrumpet to your breaſt:
The Fleſh is next, which in fruition waſtes,
High fluſh'd with all the ſenſual joys it taſtes;   50
While men the fair the goodly ſoul deſtroy,
From whence the Fleſh has pow'r to taſte a joy.
Seek thou Religion primitively found——
Well, gentle Friend! but where may ſhe be found?

Know thy foes: the foul Devil (he whom thou
Striv'ſt to pleaſe) for hate, not love, would allow
Thee fain his whole realm to be quit; and as
The world's all parts wither away and paſs,
So the World's ſelf, thy other lov'd foe, is
In her decrepit wane, and thou loving this
Doſt love a withered and worn ſtrumpet: laſt   39
Fleſh ſelf's death) and joyes which fleſh can taſt
Thou loveſt; and thy fair goodly ſoul, which doth
Give this fleſh power to taſt joy, thou doſt loath.
Seek true Religion! O where? Mirreus
Thinking her unhous'd here, and fled from us,

By faith implicit blind Ignaro led,   55
Thinks the bright feraph from his country fled,
And feeks her feat at Rome, becaufe we know
She there was feen a thoufand years ago,
And loves her relic rags, as men obey
The foot-cloth where the prince fat yefterday.   60
Thefe pageant forms are whining Obed's fcorn,
Who feeks Religion at Geneva born ;
A fullen thing, whofe coarfenefs fuits the crowd,
Tho' young unhandfome; tho' unhandfome proud.
Thus, with the wanton, fome perverfely judge
All girls unhealthy but the country drudge.   66
   No foreign fchemes make eafy Cæpio roam,
The man contented takes his church at home;

Seeks her at Rome: there, becaufe he doth know
That fhe was there a thoufand years ago,
He loves the raggs fo, as we here obey
The ftate-cloth where the prince fate yefterday.
Grants to fuch brave loves will not be inthrall'd,
But loves her only who at Geneva is call'd
Religion, plain, fimple, fullen, young,
Contemptuous yet unhandfome. As among
Lecherous humours there is one that judges
No wenches wholfome but courfe country drudges.
Grajus ftayes ftill at home here, and becaufe
Some preachers, vile ambitious bawds, and laws

Nay, fhould fome preachers, fervile bawds of gain,
Should fome new laws, which like new fafhions reign,
Command his faith to count falvation ty'd   71
To vifit his, and vifit none befide, ·
He grants falvation centres in his own,
And grants it centres but in his alone :
From youth to age he grafps the proffer'd dame, 75
And they confer his faith who give his name;
So from the guardians' hands the wards who live
Enthrall'd to guardians take the wives they give.
   From all profeffions carelefs Airy flies,
For all profeffions can't be good, he cries;   80
And here a fault, and there another views,
And lives unfix'd for want of heart to chufe.
So men, who know what fome loofe girls have done,
For fear of marrying fuch will marry none.
The charms of all obfequious Courtly ftrike,   85
On each he dotes, on each attends alike;

Still new, like fafhions, bids him think that fhe
Which dwels with us is only perfect, he
Imbraceth her whom his godfathers will
Tender to him, being tender, as wards ftill
Take fuch wives as their guardians offer or
Pay valews. Carelefs Phrygius doth abhorr
All, becaufe all cannot be good; as one
Knowing fome women whores, dares marry none.

And thinks, as different countries deck the dame,
The dreſſes altering, and the ſex the ſame :
So fares Religion, chang'd in outward ſhow,
But 'tis Religion ſtill where'er we go.   90
This blindneſs ſprings from an exceſs of light,
And men embrace the wrong to chuſe the right.
But thou of force muſt one Religion own,
And only one, and that the right alone ;
To find that right one aſk thy rev'rend ſire,   95
Let him of his, and him of his inquire:
Tho' Truth and Falſehood ſeem as twins ally'd,
There's elderſhip on Truth's delightful ſide;
Her ſeek with heed — who ſeeks the ſoundeſt firſt
Is not of no Religion, nor the worſt.   100
T' adore or ſcorn an image, or proteſt,
May all be bad. Doubt wiſely for the beſt :

Gracchus loves all as one, and thinks that ſo
As women do in divers countries go
In divers habits, yet are ſtill one kind ;
So doth, ſo is Religion ; and this blind-
Neſs too much light breeds. But unmoved thou
Of force muſt one, and forc'd but one allow,
And the right ; aſk thy father which is ſhe,
Let him aſk his. Though Truth and Falſehood be
Near twins, yet Truth a little elder is.
Be buſie to ſeek her ; believe me this,
He's not of none nor worſt that ſeeks the beſt.
To adore or ſcorn an image, or proteſt,

'Twere wrong to sleep, or headlong run astray:
It is not wand'ring to inquire the way.

On a large mountain, at the basis wide,   105
Steep to the top, and craggy at the side,
Sits sacred Truth enthron'd; and he who means
To reach the summit, mounts with weary pains,
Winds round and round, and every turn essays,
Where sudden breaks resist the shorter ways.   110
Yet labour so, that ere faint age arrive,
Thy searching soul possess her rest alive.
To work by twilight were to work too late,
And age is twilight to the night of Fate.
To will alone is but to mean delay ;   115
To work at present is the use of day:
For man's employ much thought and deed remain,
High thoughts the soul, hard deeds the body strain,

May all the bad. Doubt wisely : in strange way
To stand inquiring right is not to stray:
To sleep or run wrong is. On a huge hill,
Cragged and steep, Truth stands, and he that will
Reach her, about must and about it go;
And what the hill's suddenness resists, win so,
Yet strive so, that before age, death's twilight,
Thy soul rest ; for none can work in that night.
To will implyes delay, therefore now do.
Hard deeds the bodies pains ; hard knowledge to
The mind's indeavours reach ; and mysteries
Are like the sun, dazling, yet plain to all eyes.

And myft'ries afk believing, which to view,
  Like the fair fun, are plain, but dazzling too.   120
    Be truth, fo found, with facred heed poffeft,
Not kings have power to tear it from thy breaft.
By no blank charters harm they where they hate,
Nor are they vicars, but the hands of Fate.
Ah! fool and wretch! who lett'ft thy foul be ty'd 125
To human laws! or muft it fo be try'd?
Or will it boot thee, at the lateft day,
When Judgment fits, and Juftice afks thy plea,
That Philip that, or Greg'ry taught thee this,
Or John or Martin? All may teach amifs;   130
For ev'ry contrary in fuch extreme
This holds alike, and each may plead the fame.
    Wouldft thou to pow'r a proper duty fhow?
'Tis thy firft tafk the bounds of Power to know,

Keep the truth which thou haft found; men do not ftand
In fo ill cafe that God hath with his hand
Sign'd kings blank charters to kill whom they hate,
Nor are they vicars, but hangmen to Fate.
Fool and wretch! wilt thou let thy foul be tyed
To man's laws, by which fhe fhall not be tryed
At the laft day? or will it then boot thee
To fay a Philip or a Gregory,
A Harry or a Martin, taught me this?
Is not this excufe for meer contraries
Equally ftrong? cannot both fides fay fo?   [know,
That thou mayeft rightly obey Power, her bounds

The bounds once paſt, it holds the ſame no more, 135
Its nature alters, which it own'd before;
Nor were ſubmiſſion humbleneſs expreſt,
But all a low idolatry at beſt.
Pow'r from above, ſubordinately ſpread,
Streams like a fountain from th' eternal head;   140
There calm and pure the living waters flow,
But roars a torrent or a flood below;
Each flow'r ordain'd the margins to adorn,
Each native beauty from its roots is torn,
And left on deſerts, rocks, and ſands, are toſt,   145
All the long travel, and in ocean loſt.
So fares the ſoul which more that power reveres
Man claims from God, than what in God inheres. 148

Thoſe paſt her nature and name are chang'd; to be
Then humble to her is idolatry.
As ſtreams are power is: thoſe beſt flowers that dwell
At the rough ſtream's calm head thrive and do well;
But having left their roots, and themſelves given
To the ſtream's tyrannous rage, alas! are driven
Through mills, rocks, and woods, and at laſt, almoſt
Conſum'd in going. in the ſea are loſ' :
So periſh ſouls which more chuſe men's unjuſt
Power, from God claim'd, then God himſelf to truſt.

5

TO THE READER.

THE following Poems were given by the Author to the late Benjamin Everard, Esq. and since his death found by his son among several other valuable manuscripts, who gave them to the Editor. The receipt annexed in Dean Swift's own hand-writing, and found at the same time, shews an acknowledgment that they are actually genuine.

•

Dec. 5. 1723.

Then received from Benjamin Everard, Esq. the above writings of the late Doctor Parnell, in four stitched volumes of manuscript, which I promise to restore to him on demand. JONATHAN SWIFT.

The Editor finds himself obliged, in gratitude to the memory of the Author, thus to introduce these Posthumous Works †, lest they might be doubted really his. The former Poems, published in his lifetime, were justly admired

---

† The whole of the following Poems, to the end of Vol. II. fall under the denomination of *The Posthumous Works of Dr. Thomas Parnell*, late Arch-deacon of Clogher, containing Poems moral and divine, and on various other subjects; which were collected together, and published in one volume octavo.——The Hymns to Morning, Noon, and Evening, made also part of that Posthumous publication, but are printed in the preceding part of this volume, under the general title of *Hymns*, agreeable to the arrangement observed throughout the whole of these volumes of *The Poets of Great Britain*, by which each particular species of poetry will be found classed under its proper head.——The poem of the Horse and the Olive, and the Versification of the Third Satire of Dr. Donne, by our Author, are to be found only in this edition of Dr. Parnell's Poems.

Volume I. N

by all judges of poetry and literature, and highly com-
mended by the late Mr. Pope, in his Dedication to the
Earl of Oxford, beginning thus :

Such were the notes thy once-lov'd Poet fung,
Till Death untimely ftopp'd his tuneful tongue.
Oh ! juft beheld and loft ! admir'd and mourn'd !
With fofteft manners, gentleft arts, adorn'd !
Blefs'd in each fcience ! blefs'd in every ftrain !
Dear to the Mufe, to Harley dear----in vain !----
    Abfent or dead, ftill let a friend be dear,
(A figh the abfent claims, the dead a tear)
Recall thofe nights that clos'd thy toilfome days,
Still hear thy Parnell in his living lays.

Such were the fentiments of Mr. Pope, but, alas! he is no
more to fing the praifes of his Parnell ! How weak the
pencil of praife in any but the hands of fuch a mafter !
therefore I leave to my readers how far thefe Productions
come up to, if not excel, any of his former, being ac-
tuated, or rather divinely infpired, in the following fub-
jects, fo far as relates to the Holy Scriptures. Having
then the honour to ufher this Orphan into the world, my
heart exults in fure and permanent hope that the Father
now tunes his lyre in the celeftial fpheres in harmony of
numbers.

THE GIFT OF POETRY.

From realms of never-interrupted peace,
From thy fair ſtation near the throne of Grace,
From choirs of angels, joys in endleſs round,
And endleſs Harmony's enchanting ſound,
Charm'd with a zeal the Maker's praiſe to ſhow,   5
Bright Gift of Verſe deſcend! and here below
My raviſh'd heart with rais'd affection fill,
And warbling o'er the ſoul incline my will.
Among thy pomp let rich Expreſſion wait,
Let ranging Numbers form thy train complete,   10
While at thy motions over all the ſky
Sweet ſounds, and echoes ſweet, reſounding fly;
And where thy feet with gliding beauty tread,
Let Fancy's flow'ry ſpring erect its head.
    It comes, it comes with unaccuſtom'd light!   15
The tracts of airy thought grow wondrous bright;
Its notions ancient Memory reviews,
And young Invention new deſigns purſues;
To ſome attempt my will and wiſhes preſs,
And pleaſure, rais'd in hope, forbodes ſucceſs.   20
My God! from whom proceed the gifts divine,
My God! I think I feel the gift is thine.
Be this no vain illuſion which I find,
Nor Nature's impulſe on the paſſive mind,
But Reaſon's act, produc'd by good deſire,   25
By grace enliven'd with celeſtial fire;

While bafe conceits, like mifty fons of Night,
Before fuch beams of glory take their flight,
And frail affections, born of earth, decay,
Like weeds that wither in the warmer ray.   30

  I thank thee, Father! with a grateful mind,
Man's undeferving, and thy mercy kind;
I now perceive I long to fing thy praife,
I now perceive I long to find my lays,
The fweet incentives of another's love,   35
And fure fuch longings have their rife above;
My refolution ftands confirm'd within,
My lines afpiring eagerly begin;
Begin, my Lines! to fuch a fubject due,
That aids our labours and rewards them too;   40
Begin, while Canaan opens to mine eyes,
Where fouls and fongs divinely form'd arife.

  As one whom o'er the fweetly-vary'd meads
Entire recefs and lonely pleafure leads,
To verdur'd banks, to paths adorn'd with flowers, 45
To fhady trees, to clofely-waving bowers,
To bubbling fountains, and afide the ftream
That foftly gliding fooths a waking dream,
Or bears the thought infpir'd with heat along,
And with fair images improves a fong;   50
Thro' facred anthems fo may Fancy range,
So ftill from beauty ftill to beauty change,
To feel delights in all the radiant way,
And with fweet numbers what it feels repay:

For this I call that ancient Time appear,   55
And bring his rolls to ferve in method here;
His rolls, which acts that endlefs honour claim   ,
Have rank'd in order for the voice of Fame.   (

  My call is favour'd, Time, from firft to laft, .
Unwinds his years; the prefent fees the paft: 60
I view their circles as he turns them o'er,
And fix my footfteps where he went before.

  The page unfolding would a top difclofe,
Where founds melodious in their birth arofe;
Where firft the morning ftars together fung,   65
Where firft their harps the fons of glory ftrung
With fhouts of joy, while hallelujahs rife
To prove the chorus of eternal fkies;
Rich fparkling ftrokes the letters doubly gild,
And all's with love and admiration fill'd.   70

THE SOUL IN SORROW.

WITH kind compaſſion hear my cry,
O Jeſu! Lord of life, on high!
As when the ſummer's ſeaſons beat
With ſcorching flame and parching heat,
The trees are burnt, the flowers fade,   5
And thirſty gaps in earth are made,
My thoughts of comfort languiſh ſo,
And ſo my ſoul is broke by woe.
Then on thy ſervant's drooping head
Thy dews of bleſſing ſweetly ſhed;   10
Let thoſe a quick refreſhment give,
And raiſe my mind, and bid me live.
My fears of danger while I breathe,
My dread of endleſs hell beneath,
My ſenſe of ſorrow for my ſin,   15
To ſpringing comfort change within;
Change all my ſad complaints for eaſe,
To cheerful notes of endleſs praiſe,
Nor let a tear mine eyes employ,
But ſuch as owe their birth to joy;   20
Joy tranſporting, ſweet and ſtrong,
Fit to fill and raiſe my ſong;
Joy that ſhall reſounded be
While days and nights ſucceed for me.
Be not as a judge ſevere,   25
For ſo thy preſence who may bear?

On all my words and actions look,
(I know they're written in thy book)
But then regard my mournful cry,
And look with Mercy's gracious eye: 30
What needs my blood, since thine will do
To pay the debt to justice due?
O tender Mercy's art divine!
Thy sorrow proves the cure of mine;
Thy dropping wounds, thy woful smart, 35
Allay the bleedings of my heart:
Thy death, in death's extreme of pain,
Restores my soul to life again.
Guide me, then, for here I burn
To make my Saviour some return. 40
I'll rise, (if that will please him still,
And sure I've heard him own it will)
I'll trace his steps and bear my cross,
Despising ev'ry grief and loss,
Since he, despising pain and shame,
First took up his, and did the same. 45

THE HAPPY MAN.

How bless'd the man, how fully so,
As far as man is bless'd below,
Who, taking up his cross, essays
To follow Jesus all his days,

With resolution to obey,   5
And steps enlarging in his way!
The Father of the saints above
Adopts him with a father's love,
And makes his bosom throughly shine
With wondrous stores of grace divine;   10
Sweet grace divine, the pledge of joy,
That will his soul above employ;
Full joy, that when his time is done
Becomes his portion as a son.
Ah me! the sweet infus'd desires,   15
The fervid wishes, holy fires,
Which thus a melted heart refine,
Such are his, and such be mine.
From hence despising all besides
That earth reveals or ocean hides,   20
All that men in either prize,
On God alone he sets his eyes:
From hence his hope is on the wings,
His health renews, his safety springs,
His glory blazes up below,   25
And all the streams of comfort flow.
   He calls his Saviour King above,
Lord of Mercy, Lord of Love,
And finds a kingly care defend,
And Mercy smile, and Love descend   30
To cheer, to guide him in the ways
Of this vain world's deceitful maze:

And tho' the wicked earth difplay
Its terrors in their fierce array,
Or gape fo wide that horror fhows   35
'Tis hell replete with endlefs woes;
Such fuccour keeps him clear of ill,
Still firm to good, and dauntlefs ftill.
So, fix'd by Providence's hands,
A rock amidft an ocean ftands;   40
So bears, without a trembling dread,
The tempeft beating round its head,
And with its fide repels the wave
Whofe hollow feems a coming grave:
The fkies, the deeps, are heard to roar,   45
The rock ftands fettled as before.
　　I, all with whom he has to do,
Admire the life which bleffes you,
That feeds a foe. that aids a friend,
Without a bve-defigning end;   50
Its knowing real int'reft lies
On the bright fide of yonder fkies,
Where, having made a title fair,
It mounts, and leaves the world to Care,
While he that feeks for pleafing days   55
In earthly joys and evil ways,
Is but the fool of Toil or Fame,
(Tho' happy be the fpacious name)
And made by wealth, which makes him great,
A more confpicuous wretch of ftate.   60

THE WAY TO HAPPINESS.

How long, ye miferable blind!
Shall idle dreams engage your mind?
How long the paffions make their flight
At empty fhadows of delight?
No more in paths of error ftray,
The Lord, thy Jefus, is the way,
The fpring of happinefs; and where
Should men feek happinefs but there?
Then run to meet him at your need,
Run with boldnefs, run with fpeed,
For he forfook his own abode
To meet thee more than half the road.
He laid afide his radiant crown,
And love for mankind brought him down
To thirft and hunger, pain and woe,
To wounds, to death itfelf, below;
And he that fuffer'd thefe alone
For all the world, defpifes none.
To bid the foul that's fick be clean,
To bring the loft to life again,
To comfort thofe that grieve for ill,
Is his peculiar goodnefs ftill.
And as the thoughts of parents run
Upon a dear and only fon,

So kind a love his mercies ſhow,   25
So kind, and more extremely ſo.
   Thrice happy Men! (or find a phraſe
That ſpeaks your bliſs with greater praiſe)
Who, moſt obedient to thy call,
Leaving pleaſures, leaving all,   30
With heart, with ſoul, with ſtrength, incline,
O ſweeteſt Jeſu! to be thine.
Who know thy will, obſerve thy ways,
And in thy ſervice ſpend their days,
E'en death, that ſeems to ſet them free,
But brings them cloſer ſtill to thee.   36

THE CONVERT'S LOVE.

Bₗₑₛₛₑₚ Light of ſaints on high,
Who fill the manſions of the ſky;
Sure Defence, whoſe mercy ſtill
Preſerves thy ſubjects here from ill;
O my Jeſus! make me know   5
How to pay the thanks I owe.
   As the fond ſheep that idiely ſtrays
With wanton play thro' winding ways,
Which never hits the road of home,
O'er wilds of danger learns to roam,   10
Till wearied out with idle fear,
And paſſing there and turning here, -

He will for reſt to covert run,
And meet the wolf he wiſh'd to ſhun :
Thus wretched I, thro' wanton will   15
Run blind and headlong on in ill :
'Twas thus from ſin to ſin I flew,
And thus I might have periſh'd too,
But Mercy dropt the likeneſs here,
And ſhew'd and ſav'd me from my fear ;   20
While o'er the darkneſs of my mind
The ſacred Spirit purely ſhin'd,
And mark'd and bright'ned all the way
Which leads to everlaſting day,
And broke the thick'ning clouds of ſin,   25
And fix'd the light of love within.

    From hence my raviſh'd ſoul aſpires,
And dates the riſe of its deſires :
From hence to thee, my God! I turn,
And fervent wiſhes ſay I burn ;   30
I burn thy glorious face to ſee,
And live in endleſs joy with thee.

    There's no ſuch ardent kind of flame
Between the lover and the dame ;
Nor ſuch affection parents bear   35
To their young and only heir,
Tho' join'd together both conſpire,
And boaſt a doubled force of fire :
My tender heart within its ſeat
Diſſolves before the ſcorching heat,   40

As soft'ning wax is taught to run
Before the warmness of the sun.

O my flame, my pleasing pain,
Burn and purify my stain !
Warm me, burn me, day by day,
Till you purge my earth away,
Till at the last I throughly shine,
And turn a torch of love divine.

A DESIRE TO PRAISE.

Propitious Son of God ! to thee
With all my soul I bend my knee ;
My wish I send, my want impart,
And dedicate my mind and heart ;
For as an absent parent's son,
Whose second year is only run,
When no protecting friend is near,
Void of wit, and void of fear,
With things that hurt him fondly plays,
Or here he falls, or there he strays ;
So, should my soul's eternal guide,
The sacred Spirit, be deny'd,
Thy servant soon the loss would know,
And sink in sin, or run to woe.

O Spirit ! bountifully kind,
Warm, possess, and fill my mind ;

Difperfe my fins with light divine,
And raife the flames of love with thine:
Before thy pleafures rightly priz'd,
Let wealth and honour be defpis'd,   20
And let the Father's glory be
More dear itfelf than life to me.

   Sing of Jefus, Virgins! fing
Him your everlafting King;
Sing of Jefus, cheerful Youth!   25
Him the God of love and truth :
Write and raife a fong divine,
Or come and hear, and borrow mine.
Son eternal! Word fupreme!
Who made the univerfal frame,   30
Heav'n, and all its fhining fhow,
Earth, and all it holds below,
Bow with mercy, bow thine ear,
While we fing thy praifes here.
Son eternal! ever bleft,   35
Refting on the Father's breaft,
Whofe tender love for all provides,
Whofe power over all prefides,
Bow with pity, bow thine ear,
While we fing thy praifes here.   40
   Thou, by Pity's foft extreme
Mov'd, and won, and fet on flame,
Affum'd the form of man, and fell
In pains to refcue man from hell.

How bright thine humble glories rife;   45
And match the luftre of the fkies!
From death and hell's dejected ftate
Arifing, thou refum'd thy feat,
And golden thrones of blifs prepar'd
Above, to be thy faints' reward.   50
  How bright thy glorious honours rife,
And with new luftre grace the fkies!
For thee the fweet feraphic choir
Raife the voice and tune the lyre,
And praifes with harmonious founds .   55
Thro' all the higheft heav'n rebounds.
  O make our notes with theirs agree,
And blefs the fouls that fing of thee.
To thee the churches here rejoice,
The folemn organs aid the voice :   60
To facred roofs the found we raife,
The facred roofs refound thy praife;
And while our notes in one agree,
O blefs the church that fings to thee!   64

ON HAPPINESS IN THIS LIFE.

THE morning opens very freshly gay,
And life itself is in the month of May.
With green my fancy paints an arbour o'er,
And flow'rets with a thousand colours more,
Then falls to weaving that, and spreading these, 5
And softly shakes them with an easy breeze;
With golden fruit adorns the bending shade,
Or trails a silver water o'er its bed.
Glide, gentle Water! still more gently by,
While in this summer-bower of bliss I lie,   10
And sweetly sing of sense-delighting flames,
And nymphs' and shepherds' soft-invented names,
Or view the branches which around me twine,
And praise their fruit, diffusing sprightly wine;
Or find new pleasures in the world to praise, 15
And still with this return adorn my lays;
" Range round your gardens of eternal spring;
" Go range, my Senses! while I sweetly sing."
    In vain, in vain, alas! seduc'd by ill,
And acted wildly by the force of will,   20
I tell my soul it will be constant May,
And charm a season never made to stay;
My beauteous arbour will not stand a storm,
The world but promises, and can't perform:
Then fade, ye Leaves! and wither, all ye Flow'rs! 25
I'll dote no longer in enchanted bow'rs,

But sadly mourn, in melancholy song,
The vain conceits that held my soul so long,
The lusts that tempt us with delusive show,
And sin, brought forth for everlasting woe.   30
Thus shall the notes to sorrow's object rise,
While frequent rests procure a place for sighs;
And as I moan upon the naked plain,
Be this the burthen closing ev'ry strain;
" Return, my Senses! range no more abroad;
" He'll only find his bliss who seeks for God."   36

ECSTASY.

The fleeting joys which all affords below
Work the fond heart with unperforming show,
The wish that makes our happier life complete,
Nor grasps the wealth nor honours of the great,
Nor loosely sails on Pleasure's easy stream,   5
Nor gathers wreaths from all the groves of Fame;
Weak Man! who charms to these alone confine,
Attend my pray'r, and learn to make it thine.
    From thy rich throne, where circling trains of light
Make day that's endless infinitely bright,   10
Thence, heav'nly Father! thence with mercy dart
One beam of brightness to my longing heart:
Dawn thro' the mind, drive Error's clouds away,
And still the rage in Passion's troubled sea,

That the poor banish'd soul, serene and free,   15
May rise from earth to visit heav'n and thee.

    Come, Peace divine! shed gently from above;
Inspire my willing bosom, wondrous Love!
Thy purpled pinions to my shoulders tie,
And point the passage where I want to fly.   20

    But whither, whither now! what pow'rful fire
With this bless'd influence equals my desire?
I rise, (or Love, the kind deluder, reigns
And acts in fancy such inchanted scenes)
Earth less'ning flies, the parting skies retreat,   25
The fleecy clouds my waving feathers beat;
And now the sun, and now the stars, are gone,
Yet still methinks the spirit bears me on
Where tracts of ether purer blue display,
And edge the golden realm of native day.   30

    Oh! strange enjoyment of a bliss unseen!
Oh! ravishment! oh! sacred rage within!
Tumultuous pleasure, rais'd on peace of mind,
Sincere, excessive, from the world refin'd!
I see the light that veils the throne on high,   35
A light unpierc'd by man's impurer eye;
I hear the words that issuing thence proclaim,
" Let God's attendants praise his awful name!"
Then heads unnumber'd bend before the shrine,
Mysterious seat of Majesty divine!   40
And hands unnumber'd strike the silver string,
And tongues unnumber'd hallelujah sing.

See where the shining seraphims appear,
And sink their decent eyes with holy fear;
See flights of angels all their feathers raise,   45
And range the orbs, and as they range they praise:
Behold the great Apostles! sweetly met,
And high on pearls of azure ether set:
Behold the Prophets, full of heav'nly fire,
With wand'ring finger wake the trembling lyre;   50
And hear the Martyrs tune, and all around
The Church triumphant makes the region sound.
With harps of gold, with bows of ever-green,
With robes of white, the pious throngs are seen,
Exalted anthems all their hours employ,   55
And all is music and excess of joy.

   Charm'd with the sight, I long to bear a part,   .
The pleasure flutters at my ravish'd heart.
Sweet saints and angels of the heavenly choir!
If love has warm'd you with celestial fire,   60
Assist my words, and as they move along,
With hallelujahs crown the burthen'd song.

   Father of all above and all below,
O Great! and far beyond expression so,
No bounds thy knowledge, none thy pow'r, confine, 65
For pow'r and knowledge in their source are thine;
Around thee Glory spreads her golden wing;
Sing, glitt'ring Angels! hallelujah sing.

   Son of the Father, first begotten Son!
Ere the short measuring line of time begun,   70

The world has feen thy works, and joy'd to fee
The bright effulgence manifeft in thee.
The world muft own thee Love's unfathom'd fpring:
Sing, glitt'ring Angels! hallelujah fing.
Proceeding Spirit! equally divine,   75
In whom the Godhead's full perfections fhine,
With various graces, comforts unexpreft,
With holy tranfports you refine the breaft,
And earth is heav'nly where your gifts you bring;
Sing, glitt'ring Angels! hallelujah fing.   80
But where's my rapture, where my wondrous heat,
What interruption makes my blifs retreat?
This world's got in, the thoughts of t'other's croft,
And the gay picture's in my fancy loft.
With what an eager zeal the confcious foul   85
Would claim its feat, and foaring pafs the pole!
But our attempts thefe chains of earth reftrain,
Deride our toil, and drag us down again.
So from the ground afpiring meteors go,
And, rank'd with planets, light the world below; 90
But their own bodies fink them in the fky,
When the warmth's gone that taught them how to fly.

ON DIVINE LOVE,

BY MEDITATING ON THE WOUNDS OF CHRIST.

HOLY Jefus! God of Love!
Look with pity from above,
Shed the precious purple tide
From thine hands, thy feet, thy fide;
Let thy ftreams of comfort roll,   5
Let them pleafe and fill my foul:
Let me thus for ever be
Full of gladnefs, full of thee;
This for which my wifhes pine
Is the cup of love divine.   10
Sweet affections flow from hence,
Sweet above the joys of fenfe;
Bleffed philtre! how we find
Its facred worfhips! how the mind
Of all the world, forgetful grown,   15
Can defpife an earthly throne,
Raife its thoughts to realms above,
Think of God, and fing of love!
    Love celeftial! wondrous heat!
O beyond expreffion great!   20
What refiftlefs charms were thine
In thy good thy beft defign!
When God was hated, Sin obey'd,
And man undone without thy aid.

From the feats of endless peace   25
They brought the Son, the Lord of grace,
They taught him to receive a birth,
To clothe in flesh, to live on earth,
And after lifted him on high,
And taught him on the crofs to die.   30
   Love celeftial! ardent fire!
O extreme of fweet defire!
Spread thy brightly raging flame
Thro' and over all my frame;
Let it warm me, let it burn,   35
Let my corpfe to afhes turn,
And might thy flame thus act with me,
To fet the foul from body free,
I next would ufe thy wings, and fly
To meet my Jefus in the fky.   44

THE VISION OF PIETY.

'Twas when the night in filent fable fled,
When cheerful morning fprung with rifing red,
When dreams and vapours leave to crowd the brain,
And beft the Vifion draws its heav'nly fcene;
'Twas then, as flumb'ring on my couch I lay,   5
A fudden fplendor feem'd to kindle day,
A breeze came breathing, in a fweet perfume,
Blown from eternal gardens, fill'd the room,
And in a void of blue, that clouds inveft,
Appear'd a daughter of th' realms of Reft :   10
Her head a ring of golden glory wore,
Her honour'd hand the facred Volume bore ;
Her raiment glift'ning feem'd, a filver white,
And all her fweet companions fons of Light.
     Straight as I gaz'd my fear and wonder grew,   15
Fear barr'd my voice, and wonder fix'd my view ;
When, lo! the cherub of the fhining crowd,
That fail'd as guardian in her azure cloud,
Fann'd the foft air, and downward feem'd to glide,
And to my lips a living coal apply'd ;   20
Then while the warmth o'er all my pulfes ran,
Diffufing comfort, thus the maid began.
     " Where glorious manfions are prepar'd above,
" The feats of Mufic and the feats of Love,
" Thence I defcend, and Piety my name,   25
" To warm thy bofom with celeftial flame,

" To teach thee praifes mix'd with humble pray'rs,
" And tune thy foul to fing feraphic airs.
" Be thou my bard." A vial here fhe caught,
(An angel's hand the cryftal vial brought)   30
And, as with awful found the word was faid,
She pour'd a facred unction on my head ; .
Then thus proceeded ; " Be thy Mufe thy zeal ;
" Dare to be good, and all my joys reveal ;
" While other pencils flatt'ring forms create,   35
" And paint the gawdy plumes that deck the great ;
" While other pens exalt the vain delight,
" Whofe wafteful revel wakes the depth of night ;
" Or others foftly fing in idle lines,
" How Damon courts, or Amaryllis fhines,   40
" More wifely thou felect a theme divine,
" 'Tis flames their recompenfe, 'tis heav'n is thine.
   " Defpife the raptures of difcorded fire,
" Where wine, or paffion, or applaufe, infpire ;
" Low reftlefs life, and ravings born of earth,   45
" Whofe meaner fubjects fpeak their humble birth ;
" Like working feas, that, when loud winters blow,
" Not made for rifing, only rage below :
" Mine is a warm and yet a lambent heat,
" More lafting ftill as more intenfely great ;   50
" Produc'd where pray'r and praife and pleafure breathe,
" And ever mounting whence it fhot beneath.
" Unpaint the love that, hov'ring over beds,
" From glittering pinions guilty pleafure fheds ;

" Reftore the colour to the golden mines,   55
" With which behind the feather'd idol fhines :
" To flow'ring greens reftore their native care,
" The rofe and lily never his to wear ;
" To fweet Arabia fend the balmy breath,
" Strip the fair flefh, and call the phantom Death : 60
" His bow be fabled o'er, his fhafts the fame,
" And fork and point them with eternal flame.

 " But urge thy pow'rs, thy utmoft voice advance,
" Make the loud ftrings againft thy finger dance ;
" 'Tis love that angels praife and men adore,   65
" 'Tis love divine that afks it all and more :
" Fling back the gates of ever-blazing day,
" Pour floods of liquid light to gild the way,
" And all in glory wrapt, thro' paths untrod
" Purfue the great unfeen defcent of God ;   70
" Hail the meek Virgin, bid the Child appear,
" The Child is God ! and call him Jefus here.
" He comes ! but where to reft ? A manger's nigh ;
" Make the great Being in a manger lie.
" Fill the wide fkies with angels on the wing,   75
" Make thoufands gaze, and make ten thoufand fing.
" Let men afflict him ; men he came to fave,
" And ftill afflict him till he reach the grave.
" Make him refign'd ; his loads of forrow meet,
" And me, like Mary, weep beneath his feet ;   80
" I'll bathe my treffes there, my pray'rs rehearfe,
" And glide in flames of love along my verfe.

" Ah! while I speak I feel my bosom swell,

" My raptures smother what I long to tell!

" 'Tis God! a present God! thro' cleaving air   85

" I see the throne, and see the Jesus there

" Plac'd on the right; he shews the wounds he bore,

" (My fervours oft' have won him thus before)

" How pleas'd he looks! my words have reach'd his

" He bids the gates unbar, and calls me near." [ear,

    She ceas'd; the cloud on which she seem'd to tread

Its curls unfolded, and around her spread;   92

Bright angels waft their wings to raise the cloud,

And sweep their iv'ry lutes, and sing aloud.

The scene moves off, while all its ambient sky   95

Is turn'd to wondrous music as they fly,

And soft the swelling sounds of music grow,

And faint their softness, till they fail below.

    My downy sleep the warmth of Phœbus broke,

And while my thoughts were settling thus I spoke;

" Thou beauteous Vision! on the soul imprest,   101

" When most my reason would appear to rest,

" 'Twas sure with pencils dipt in various lights,

" Some curious angel limn'd thy sacred sights,

" From blazing suns his radiant gold he drew,   105

" While moons the silver gave, and air the blue.

" I'll mount the roving wind's expanded wing,

" And seek the sacred hill, and light to sing:

" ('Tis known in Jewry well) I'll make my lays,

" Obedient to thy summons, sound with praise.   110

" But ftill I fear, unwarm'd with holy flame,
" I take for truth the flatt'ries of a dream ;
" And barely wifh the wondrous gift I boaft,
" And faintly practice what deferves it moft.
" Indulgent Lord! whofe gracious love difplays 115
" Joys in the light, and fills the dark with eafe,
" Be this, to blefs my days, no dream of blifs,
" Or be, to blefs the nights, my dreams like this." 118

P ij

CONTENTS.

P iij

EPISTLES.

MISCELLANIES.

Page

From the APOLLO PRESS,
by the MARTINS,
March 14. 1778.

END OF VOLUME FIRST.